Underland Arcana slips through the cracks, bringing with it the numinous, the esoteric, the supernatural, and the weird. This issue contains stories about preserving planets, stories about seeking solace, stories about course catalogs, stories about strange circumstances, and stories that unfold on the periphery of consciousness. These are the stories that we shall find in the piles of dead leaves that the wind gathers as the year comes to an end.

Underland Arcana is published quarterly. This issue is published in conjunction with the new moon that comes in quietly as the leaves turn color.

EDITOR
Mark Teppo

COVER IMAGE
grandfailure

SIGIL ART
Andrew Penn Romine

PUBLISHER
Underland Press
Clackamas, OR, USA

Stand beneath the trees and let their falling leaves cover you completely . . .

https://www.underlandarcana.com

UNDERLAND ARCANA

~ 4 ~

Underland Press

Contents

The Swivel and the Pivot

Here's a story. *XVIII*, the second Major Arcana anthology, had a street date of March 17th, 2020. Yeah, I know. There was a release party scheduled for that Friday, which would have been the 20th. We went into pandemic lockdown on the 18th, and for several months, no one thought about going outside.

I was disappointed, of course, but the world did have a lot on its mind during 2020, and to get fussy about a book release getting lost in all the tragedy that was going on wasn't going to be very helpful. I did fuss, but quietly, in the eerie silence of my own home.

As it became clear we were all going to be spending a lot of time away from each other, I tried to think of a way that I could continue making tarot-themed anthologies. I certainly can't claim to be the first to think of putting up fiction online, but pivoting to that model was a way forward. If you're going to publish fiction that way, you should do it on a regular schedule, and from there, it was a hop and a skip to the idea of focusing on the Minor Arcana cards in a pocket-sized format.

Lemons to lemonade, and all that.

This is the fourth issue of that pivot. I've got a good chunk of the Minor Arcana represented already, and I hope to gather stories that will fill out the remaining fifty-six cards. I have a plan, you see . . .

It's always good to have a plan.

Anyway, we have completed our first "deck" of stories. It's important to take a moment and reflect on milestones when we reach them. I'm delighted this change in direction has been fruitful, and I look forward to building on this foundation in the years to come.

Mark Teppo
October 12th, 2021

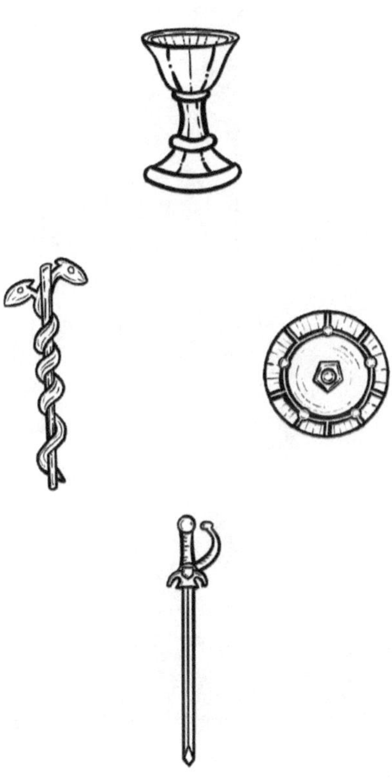

ACE of WANDS.

A Novelty of Stars

~ Brandon Crilly

He examines a polished wooden counter topped with cardstock. "Lobby cards," the outdated monitor at the front desk called them. Each black-and-white image is framed in either darkened blue, red or gold. No labels to identify them.

One near the front catches his eye. He holds it up. "Which screening is this?"

The front desk monitor pivots its head, scattering dust from its creaking joints. "Algol at Minimum Brightness, 2020," it says. Only the voice box seems to be in regular repair. "Popular."

He could almost make a shape from the pinpricks of light on the lobby card's image, but it's too worn and faded. Little better than a yellow pixelated smear. No way to know if the screen inside will have higher resolution. The theater charges enough that they'd better.

He sets the lobby card down. "Would you recommend one?"

The monitor stares out the wide, glass entrance at the shrouded sky beyond.

"Any will do," it says. "This is the only place you can see them, I am told."

V

The Lonely Box

~ Manfred Gabriel

Loneliness lurked just beyond the workbench shop light, watching as Jeff sawed and glued and nailed. He was no carpenter, but he considered himself handy, having renovated most of his century-old home himself. Still, a box was different. The sides had to be accurately measured and cut, the lid fitted so that it would close properly, could keep anything sealed inside from getting out. The last thing Jeff wanted was for his loneliness to escape.

His phone played a selection of seventies rock to keep him company, Chicago, the Eagles, the Allman Brothers. Bands he'd listened to in high school, playing on the radio as he cruised with his buddies in his Dad's lime green LTD, when he thought life would last forever and he was never, ever alone.

His friends were gone. Darren died of an aneurism at the age of forty-one. Greg lived nearby but was always busy with his new wife and a young son. Rick lived in Seattle and it had been years since they spoke. Now, the music, those memories, and working on the box were all that kept his loneliness at bay.

Finally complete, he inspected his work. The joints were tight, but the hinges took some adjustment to get it to seal. He opened and shut the lid a couple of times, flipped the latch. Not perfect, but good enough.

He took the box into the yard along with a spade. His loneliness followed at a distance, drawing nearer with each step, black against the night. Above him, the bedroom light was on, filtered through lace curtains. Janet was no doubt in her usual spot, on her side of the bed, pillows propping her up, the TV turned to some old rerun. She didn't bother to ask him what he was doing in the garage that late, didn't bother to talk to him much at all anymore. He could not say when they grew apart. It happened gradually, dinner by dinner, conversation by conversation, until, one day, he realized they were living separate lives.

The rest of the house was dark. Erik and Sonia's rooms were almost the way they'd left them when they finally moved out on their own, one after the other. Sometimes, he found himself sitting on their beds, replaying conversations from their younger days in his head. They spoke now and then over the phone, but it wasn't the same.

Jeff set the box on the patio table. If he had taken the time, he could have sanded it, maybe given it a coat of leftover varnish. It's not like he didn't have the time. Since his retirement, he had nothing but time. Raising his children, working his job, even renovating the house, had all given him purpose. Those days, how he longed to be able to rest. Now, he only wished the resting would stop.

The dog next door barked. His neighbor, Cliff or Clive, he could never remember, called the dog inside. He was a widower, had a telescope that he sometimes took out on clear nights. Other than that, Jeff knew little about the man. Over the years, they'd exchanged waves and hellos, but that was about it. There was a gate between the two houses. Who had built it and why, Jeff didn't know. It seemed it had always been there. Perhaps, once, the people in these houses had been friends, even family. The gate hadn't been used in a long time.

Jeff could feel loneliness at his back, still lurking, ready to envelope him. The idea of a box in which to keep it came to him as he was doing a long-delayed chore. He had the habit of saving the original packaging for anything he bought long after the item had broken or become obsolete and taken to recycling. Boxes for old toasters, TVs, mixers and computers cluttered a quarter of his basement. Janet had been nagging him to get rid of them, and he figured he might as well. He had nothing else to do.

As he whiled away an afternoon flattening all those boxes in a neat stack, he thought, I've kept all these boxes in case I needed to return the items kept in them. He no longer had these items. Yet, he had his loneliness, and it had to go back. Why shouldn't it have a box as well? But not some piece of reused cardboard, no, that wouldn't do. If it was to work, the box would have to be of his own making.

His loneliness crept onto his shoulders as he knew it would, as it always did when he was still, its emptiness a great weight that made it difficult to move. But move he did. He spun, snatching it before it could react, catching it unaware. It tingled in his hands as he shoved it into the box and shut the lid tight, latching it quickly so it wouldn't escape.

In Janet's garden, where tomatoes and squash and carrots were just beginning to sprout, he found a spot to bury the box. He dug deeper than he needed to and set a large rock on top it just for good measure. He refilled the hole and tamped the soil down with the back end of the spade before setting it aside.

He looked up. He used to be able to read the sky, when he was young and people still dreamed of reaching the moon. He could name each constellation, knew a planet from a star by how it failed to twinkle.

Jeff thought about his neighbor with his telescope. He went to the gate. It was covered in vines and the latch was almost rusted shut. He had to put all his weight into it to get it open.

The dog barked from inside. A light came on. His neighbor stepped onto the porch and asked who it was. Jeff answered, to the man, to the moonlight, to the shadow that was not there.

VIII

Canyon Village

~ Christi Nogle

Myra Reynolds from Canyon Village 8/16/2019 10:35
New Kid on the Block!

Just want to thank everyone for the block party a few weeks ago. Me and DH (dear hubby) and my little girl Jenny—not so little now she's fourteen lol—we all felt so welcomed! Just found out about this message board, happy to see it so active!

This must be the prettiest place I have ever lived. I just loved walking along the canyon edge, and seeing the all the fields and the distant mountains from my front door every day makes my heart SING. And you, wonderful neighbors. Being here is a dream come true.

Saul Toms from Canyon Village 8/16/2019 11:18
Re: New Kid on the Block!

Welcome, Myra!

Karen Ungular from Canyon Village 8/16/2019 18:06
Re: New Kid on the Block!

Good to see you on here Myra! Met you at the block party, remember? We're new too—just moved here in April. We're in the barn-red house right by the entry fountain—not far from you, I think. Love the whole area.

Alder Casey from Canyon Village 8/16/2019 19:35
Re: New Kid on the Block!
Welcome, Myra, Jenny, and Myra's DH!

·III·

Myra Reynolds from Canyon Village 9/20/2019 10:35
Local Legends???!!!
DD Jenny just told me there is a local legend here about a bigfoot or something. I was floored. I love that kind of thing. Tell me More!

Kendall Urrea from Canyon Village 9/20/2019 10:52
Re: Local Legends???!!!
Our family's been here sixteen years, since most of the houses were still getting built, and I haven't heard anything.

Karen Ungular from Canyon Village 9/20/2019 11:49
Re: Local Legends???!!!
Now I am curious too. Anyone know anything more? I haven't heard anything about this.

Jenn Walter-Urrea from Canyon Village 9/22/2019 19:22
Re: Local Legends???!!!

I wish, but sadly no. Just a boring subdivision. I haven't heard anything about this. Must be something the kids made up this year.

·III·

Myra Reynolds from Canyon Village 10/8/2019 10:38
Wildlife

I was wondering what kind of wildlife you'd all seen around here. DD and I have been biking out to the canyon every day this week—it's still warm enough, can't believe it! We thought we saw a fox. And there's some kind of howling we caught earlier in summer a few times. Wolves?

Joe Jennings from Burming Road West 10/9/2019 19:35
Re: Wildlife

Foxes, rabbits and other varmints, all kinds of pheasant and things like that. Coyotes and maybe coy dogs. They're the biggest things out here. I lived near here all my life and never seen a big cat anywhere this close to a town. Wolves are out of the question in most of the state. You're thinking of up north.

Myra Reynolds from Canyon Village 10/9/2019 20:07
Re: Wildlife

Thanks, Joe! Just curious, what's a coy dog??

·III·

Myra Reynolds from Canyon Village 10/11/2019 10:25
Jefferson High
[Post deleted]

Myra Reynolds from Canyon Village 10/11/2019 10:38
Jefferson High, Second Try!!

I think my post got messed up before, or maybe I did something wrong . . . Anyway, won't retype everything, but I was wondering if anyone here had had problems with bullying at Jefferson highschool. Gee, you'd think kids would be past that by this age. DD is fourteen and taller than me!!

Myra Reynolds from Canyon Village 10/13/2019 11:15
Re: Jefferson High, Second Try!!

Helooo?! How has been people's experience with Jefferson High?

Karen Ungular from Canyon Village 10/13/2019 18:55
Re: Jefferson High, Second Try!!

I didn't reply before cause my kids aren't that old yet. I don't know why people aren't answering.

*A*n*o*n*y*m*o*u*s from BFN 10/13/2019 23:58
Re: Jefferson High, Second Try!!

Maybe you ought to stop talking about your kids on here lady.

Karen Ungular, Canyon Village 10/13/2019 8:16
Re: Re: Jefferson High, Second Try!!
I didn't think this thing allowed anonymous posts???

Myra Reynolds, Canyon Village 10/13/2019 10:34
Re: Re: Re: Jefferson High, Second Try!!
And where is BFN?

Ihaventheardanythingaboutthis from Butt F***** Nowhere 10/13/2019 23:35
Re: Jefferson High, Second Try!!
Maybe you ought to stop talking on here at all lady.

·III·

10/15/2019 Recording begin time 17:38
M.R. [garbled]:—and after I pulled her out that week, she would not go back. We have her set up with online classes now, but I don't know. I'd have never thought this kind of thing would happen to her. She always got along with all kinds of kids. She was on three teams last year.

K.U.: So she was told something in confidence, and then the kids found out that she told you. She broke their confidence, but how'd they find out?

M.R.: Well, I don't know. I was asking everybody. If we saw somebody on a walk, I'd as soon as not stop and get talking. And at the market across Burming Road. She had kids over a couple times early on, and I don't think I asked them outright, but I think I might have sort of fished. If I caught them in the kitchen alone or something. You know, I think it was actually just this one girl who told Jenny. She just said it was something the kids talked about, but it had to be this girl Carlie. They really clicked at the start of the year. You know, like you and me. Going around together a little bit. It's so great when you meet a new friend right away.

K.U.: Carlie.

M.R.: You know who that is?

K.U.: I don't think so. And what all did Jenny tell you, anyway?

M.R.: I said, some sort of bigfoot thing or a missing link.

K.U. :That's all, though? She said, in her words she said that they said, "some sort of bigfoot thing or a missing link"?

M.R. [garbled]:—but yeah. That's all she said.

·Ⅲ·

Myra Reynolds, Canyon Village 10/15/2019 20:45
Thoughts and Questions
[Post deleted]

·Ⅲ·

10/17/2019 Recording begin time 18:38

M.R.: It's the kids in this neighborhood. Not all of them, but some. And the rest, they look out for them. They want them to be accepted. Like, under the radar but still accepted.

K.U.: I don't get it.

M.R.: So, the missing link things, they're all kids. They're brothers and sisters, a whole litter of them. The same age. In Jenny's grade but they don't go to school because— yeah!—because they are these twisted, distorted things. But the other kids grew up with them. They've known them since they were . . . cubs or something. Pups! They're all friends. They party with them after school and on the weekends. Party with them! They go running around in the canyons with them after dark, they bicycle after dark. She said some of them were boyfriends and girlfriends of the real kids. It's . . . Jesus, haven't you head some of this?

K.U.: I haven't heard anything about this.

M.R.: You said.

K.U.: So is that all she told you?

M.R.: Yeah? I don't know. I'm so confused. No, wait. They don't need to go to school, these things, because they're super smart. They all have these yuppie parents who have been bringing them up on like Shakespeare and chemistry sets. She said it was like that cartoon with the turtles in the sewer—or that old show I watched with her, the sexy cat man living in the sewer and there's all this candlight. Why can't I remember the name? Anyway, romantic like that . . . Oh my God, Karen. Do you think? Oh, I feel sick.

K.U.: All these yuppie parents? I thought you said they were all brothers and sisters.

M.R.: They were adopted out. Something. They found them in the canyon, or they got left on somebody's doorstep and then they got adopted out through the whole subdivi-

sion. And they're living here just barely under the radar.

K.U.: Are you saying she kept talking about it, or was it just that one time she brought this up? All of this. Myra? You there?

M.R.: Listen, I've got to go.

K.U.: Can you remember any more?

M.R.: I've got to go. Thank you, thank you, thank you for hearing me vent. It's just stupid. The kids made it up.

K.U.: This year, probably. I've asked around, and no one's heard anything.

M.R.: This year, yes. Goodbye.

·III·

10/19/2019 Recording begin time 18:14

M.R.: Carlie was leaving her alone, ever since she left school, but now it's . . . worse. Complicated. I think they're threatening her even more than she's saying. She sort of let slip that Carlie got punished for telling, but that it wasn't Carlie's fault. It was my fault. How was it my fault? I've never seen her cry so much, Karen. I'm worried. Mitch is . . . a mess, too. We're trying to keep him out of it. He's . . .

K.U.: Why did she say it was your fault?

M.R.: Because I was the one who broke the confidence. That's just how she put it.

K.U.: So Jenny did swear you to secrecy? You didn't mention that before.

M.R.: I didn't? I thought I did.

K.U.: Did you ever just think about keeping her secret?

Oh, it doesn't matter. Listen, Myra, I really like you. I want you and the whole family to be happy here. That's all anyone wants.

M.R.: I don't know. I feel kind of marked somehow, you know? I'm peeking out the blinds now. I feel weird. It feels weird here now. And Jenny won't come out of her room. She's got things piled up against her window. Like somebody's going to try to come in the window, Karen. I don't know what to do.

K.U.: Listen: The kids just randomly made this up. This year, probably. I've asked around, and no one's heard anything.

M.R.: I don't think so. That's the thing. There was so much detail. I'm so sorry I didn't tell you everything earlier. There's still more, crazy things. She says they shift, they grow all of this hair all at once. She wanted to see it. Now one of the things she cries about now, do you get it?—she cries because she says she'll never see this completely magical thing. She believes it. She had me half believing it.

K.U.: No, listen. Will you listen, Myra? Will you?

M.R.: I've been listening.

K.U.: No, please. Please. The kids just randomly made this up. This year, probably. I've asked around, and no one's heard anything. Do you understand?

M.R.: You're sweet to try to make me feel better, but I really just can't stop thinking about this. I don't know who to call, you know? Do I get her a therapist? Is there something the police could do? Contact some kid of investigator. What?

K.U.: I hear Ryan pulling up. OK, I need to go soon. You just stay calm, OK? Put something on TV and make something—or you and your honey go out somewhere nice for dinner. Whatever your favorite thing is.

M.R.: Thai. But there's no place here.

K.U.: Or Mexican. You loved the Mexican place out on Post. Order your favorite thing. You'll feel better.

M.R.: Maybe. Thank you.

K.U.: I have to go. It will be all right, OK? Jenny will be fine.

M.R.: Thank you. Bye bye. [ends call]

K.U.: Shit.

·III·

John Folger from Canyon Village 2/10/2020 15:12
Your New Neighbor!

Just want to say hi to everybody after the amazing block party! We just moved into the gray two-story across from the fountain. As a stay-at-home dad, I am overjoyed to have come to such a welcoming neighborhood.

Saul Toms from Canyon Village 2/10/2020 18:00
Re: Your New Neighbor

Glad to have you, John! I am a stay-at-home dad too. Dipping our toe into homeschooling this year. Looking forward to getting to know you.

Karen Ungular from Canyon Village 2/10/2020 18:06
Re: Your New Neighbor!

Nice to meet you John! Met you at the block party, remember? We're new too—just moved here in April.

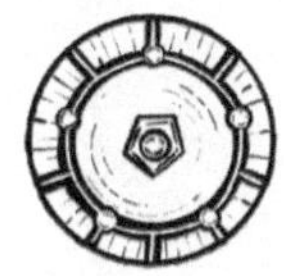

Night Harrowing

~ *Catherine Hansen*

Easter, who was three, was trying to climb onto my back while I did pushups. It delighted her how I groaned and teetered but did not stop. Mommy was weak yet Mommy was strong.

I had long since stopped leaving our apartment during the day. Except when I bore my daughter's weight, I hardly felt I was myself. And these repetitive movements—pushing, lifting—were a way of dwelling in this flimsy body, confessing that it was still my own. I savored it like the company of someone I planned to jilt.

Sometimes I kept pushing up until my arms shook and gave way, and I lay there stunned and annoyed while Easter crowed. In the other place, in the other body, nothing could tire me.

When I first started harrowing hell, it was on the night shift. It was a second job like any single mother might take when ends are not meeting. One famed harrower, the monk Ksitigarbha, is supposed to have refused nirvana just on the edge of reaching it. It was unthinkable to scale the heavens until the hells and all their seas were empty of suffering and their inhabitants freed. If I don't go to help them, he said, who will? I never glimpsed or refused enlightenment. No ends had met. I had no idea what I was doing.

The day it began, I was home with Easter on a weekday holiday. For much of the morning, as I caught up on chores long postponed, she had pressed for my attention. Life with her was often a matter of two irreconcilable sets of priorities, grinding their gears. Now, as the early drizzle turned to a hard rain, she was playing with her toys on her cork mat and I was listening to the cozy burble of their imaginary conversation.

"Yes please, I would like to have a birthday!" said a stuffed dragon.

"Then we must bake a cake," said an owl.

Suddenly, I felt watched. Rather, I felt framed by an awareness that was not mine. The sensation sharpened. I knew in the way I know in dreams: something had cast and cast about for me, and then had fixed upon me, and now already was coming for me. Full cry, headlong, it grew in my inner vision and filled it. And then it replaced me. There was no other word for what I felt. I had been replaced.

An observer might have noticed nothing, and my daughter didn't even look up.

In a fraction of that second's sleight of hand, another mind had stirred beside mine. A fraction after that, it was extinguished. Someone's will or emotion had risen and thrashed, like a shape under bedsheets—surprise, triumph, or shock—and now it was gone.

But it had left something behind, at the back of me.

My inner surface followed its curves, as if I were a mask upon a scowling face. I was now a mere shadow of a thing more real.

"Mommy?" said my daughter. I had been silent too long. Swinging my chair around, I heaved her to my lap. I hugged her as she squirmed and tried to gather my thoughts as they scattered.

All the following morning as I made our breakfast and laid out our two sets of clothes, and then all day at work, it was there—my real body. That was the phrase that rose eerily in my mind. I tried to live our life for us like before, dropping Easter off at daycare on the way to my crowded desk. But its presence rang in my ears like a key struck deep down the scale, the minor note that darkens the chord. It was late November, and night by five. Among the last to leave work, caught in the amber of the last lighted floor, I seemed to see my real body one floor below, in the dark – mirroring my movements down the halls, stooping through the doorways.

One night I finally reached back for the thing that was reaching for me. After Easter was asleep, I locked myself in the bathroom. What I did then, with a frightful minimum of effort, was like closing one eye and opening another. Very suddenly my shoulders filled the tiny, lightless room as bottles clattered from shelves. As my head bent against the low ceiling, I thought I heard my daughter calling for me. First I froze. Then I recoiled in every way I knew how, trying to escape without daring to look down at what I was escaping from, but nothing changed. I was a hand jerking back from a hot pan, but the hand would not move. The matter of minutes it must have taken to return to myself passed for eternity.

Twenty-four hours later, I cowered in the foyer with my back to the shoe cabinet and did it again. I revolved slowly in the half-mirror that rattled on the hall door, turning my head as dancers do to keep vertigo at bay. Easter wasn't sleep-talking this time, but at the faintest noise from outside I was already clawing myself back, hysterical and guilty. Easter's mother's body was still right there, slipped into an adjacent, invisible slice of space. But it eluded the grasp, like a bar of soap in bathwater. It was not forthcoming. My real body was.

On the third night, the low clouds glowed with city lights. I was gaping in the tottery mirror at something that resembled large black ferns adhering to my back, busily overlapping from neck to waist. Bending over to study my real face had made me faint and sick. Nothing prevented my daughter from simply waking up, opening the door, and coming barefoot and dazed to look for me—the huge, jagged, cringing shadow in the corner. We would have to face each other in mutual terror, or she would just bolt senselessly for refuge in my arms, finding me nowhere until at last I flickered back.

The thought was unbearable, and so I decided I had to strike out alone. The city was a glowing dome with darkness pressing in all around it, and I imagined I had to get to that darkness. I found a babysitter and told him I was helping a friend's band record an album: a story he could have done without, as it wore thin over the weeks.

I didn't have a car. I took a late train one night into the city's upland outskirts, got off at the last little unmanned station, and chose a street that meandered uphill. The dark display of a closed shop framed the last streetlight. At the last house, the one lit window displayed a row of near-empty detergent bottles. The road turned steep and gravelly, switchbacking up for a mile or more to arrive at a deserted field, where a lonely sodium lamp gilded a pit full of planks and rebar. The field's far edge lay in the deep shadow of trees.

I had only been in my real body for minutes at a time. The first thing I thought to do with it now was to speak. Squatting in the dark under the trees, I heard its voice for the first time, and I was enchanted. It was thunderously deep. Every neutral phrase I tried to utter was heightened and haughty, a stage villain's repartee. I talked just to keep hearing it.

"My name is Griet," said my colossal, pitch-black voice, several times.

"I have a baby," it said. "Bay-by." I started to giggle and stopped short.

"I think I'm going to find out if I can fly," I said out loud to myself. I had guessed that the fronds on my back—pleated in intricate shrink-wrap patterns—might be wings. Since I had no idea how to make them function that way, I walked instead, and ran, and loped in circles. I broke a stone by crushing it in my left hand.

That moment of disconcerting triumph gave me pause. I saw with what half-conscious intensity I had been seeking something to crush. Insights, instincts, and desires lay tightly folded in every exploratory movement I had made. Now, under my silent self-regard, they loosened and drifted dimly before me. This thing, in whose reality I dwelled, was combative and proud. It hummed with anger and delighted in violence. It might find its truth roaring with joy astride vast ruins.

If I saw no place for that in my life, then I had no business returning to the field the following night, and then night after night. Yet I did—appalled and exultant.

Soon I started trying to photograph myself. I became fixated on one shot in particular.

It cut me off at the ankles and across the forehead as I crouched awkwardly and hugged my shoulders to fit my whole frame in. The lips drew back in an involuntary snarl at the flash, and the eyes lit up like a cave pool a mile beneath the earth. For a time, I was more in love with myself, specifically as I appeared in that photo, than with anyone I'd ever been with. I burned with the thought of myself. Sometimes I imagined being shown off like statuary: standing counterpoised, at my full height, with the extravagant crests like some ferocious ornamental bird and the smile full of murderous teeth. My imagination embarrassed me—like someone who casually alludes to a secret obsession in conversation, and feels the blazing glory rise to his cheeks. To this day, if it is a day at all, I am afraid that somehow I chose this, or that I brought it on myself.

Sometimes Easter freed me. When I picked her up every afternoon, holding her hand on the way to the station, I felt calm and empty. As she stopped at every pretext, to exclaim over a puddle or throw handfuls of leaves, I had no desire to be anything but the thing she called, the thing she called into being over and over, when she said "Mommy."

But the night field took on irrational, ritual contours in my mind, lost in the mountainous dark that pressed upon the dome of light. It was like going to see a lover. I blew my strained budget many times over on the babysitter and the train, and lost untold hours of sleep.

One night, I found a rusting utility trailer in the woods around the field. I thought of nothing better to do than to pick it up and throw it down a ravine, like a teenager trying to impress his girlfriend. As I did, a broken spar of it gashed my side. When I looked at what I had done to myself I was paralyzed. I had wrecked something I didn't know how to fix. That is when I noticed that the pennons on my back had partially separated, and hung like wet, black saran wrap. I had insulted my body by injuring it, I thought in my rising fright. Now it was going to fall to pieces in self-destructive vengeance. I tried gingerly to touch the place under my ribs, but misjudged the distance and instead thrust two serrated talons right into the bleeding flesh. My body roared at me through my own mouth with rage and hurt. Now it was clear I was disintegrating: I couldn't see my legs anymore. I was standing on vapor, wading in it. Panicking, I fled myself like a sinking ship.

As I returned by train that early dawn, unable to doze, I knew my body was a shattered ruin. I thought I could wait until nightfall to be sure of it, but I was so desperate to learn what had become of me that I did it in the bathroom at work that day, right in the open because the stalls were too small. And there I was, over the row of sinks, stark in the tawdry light. Utterly whole and restored, rueful and smirking, heedless of passing footsteps in the hall—the being in the mirror was, for all I knew, imperishable.

Several nights later I deliberately injured myself to see what would happen. The effect was immediate. At my back, the fern fronds separated again and hung in damp webs. Now my legs were gone; I was waist deep in a fog driven by wind, and this time I waited. The fog rose, and took me with it. After that, I was somewhere else.

I saw bare slopes, red like the threat of fire. A vacant phrase rose in my mind: the other side. At that time I still understood nothing, but that is exactly what it was. One of the other sides. As if I had emerged from a chrysalis, my wings (this is exactly what they were) stirred at my back, then briskly rose and tautened. Taking first flight felt like a new species of emotion, borne up by the landscape. The land sustained me because it knew me. It knew where I was from and what I was for.

I planed high over billows of earth mottled red and black. I began to see helpless bodies rolling in the heavy swell, as winged forms circled above—coal-shaded scars on the low sky. There was so much I didn't understand then: that this vast shipwreck with its circling raptors was mere appearance, a sediment of myth; but that its brutish matter repelled the meaning made by myths; and that both of these were true to say. Twisting bodies pushed up from deep in the red, curdled earth, to collapse exhausted and be carried away to the pits. Yet these bodies were immaterial, invisible. The pits, crammed full of limbs and lament, were also empty holes in the ground. The immaterial bodies were here for reasons they would never know. For reasons of justice, for reasons forgotten and long superseded, for inane or for implacably logical reasons.

The winged creatures, who looked like me, swooped down here and there like unwieldy peregrines to attend to the bodies. They took heavy flight again, or fell casually on each other, rending and maiming. They did not know the reasons either.

I landed at the crumbling edge of a pit. Petals in a broken thicket, the faces turned up in unison. Reaching down thoughtlessly to take the hand of the nearest one, I forgot myself until I saw that the others were trying to bury themselves and hide from me. The man struggled too, but I would not let go of his hand, and he went slack as I worked him free. As I folded him in my arms, he began to shake, and I shook too. There was nowhere else to go, nowhere to carry this body with its wobbling head and moaning mouth.

Some of the winged figures had stopped short in their orbit around the pits that pocked the earth into the endless distance. They were heading toward us. One of them paused low above us in tightening gyres. I laid the man between my feet just as it fell to the attack, clawing at my shoulders as I shielded the body beneath me. When I turned, and gripped the jaws of the creature at my back, and tore, and kept tearing as it buffeted me with desperate wings, I didn't think to wonder why I could do such things. I should have. When it was over I only stared at what I had destroyed, drawing the fading rapture close around me like a squalid mantle. Then I was certain I had made a terrible mistake—that I had let myself feel and do something ghastly, and now I was trapped, and lost. I groped in emptiness for my old, my own, my kindly shape, as I would have done in the field, ready to jog back down to the station. It wasn't there.

It was the man I was trying to rescue who showed me the way back out. I had gathered him up again and was cradling him to my chest. His knees were drawn up and his eyes were tightly closed. My mind kept helplessly reaching, and finally it touched something. It didn't belong to me, but to him. It was close by us, though he surely could not have known it existed, as perhaps it always had. Right then, because I perceived that I could, I spread my wings and simply stepped across to where it waited.

Tall grass surrounded me, under a muted sky the color of a long-postponed sunrise. I was no longer carrying anyone.

The man stood across from me, on unbroken legs, gazing at me with a strange expression as if he understood something vast. Then he simply turned and walked away, parting the grass.

This was not earth, nor the hell we had come from. It was a silken fringe springing like sedge from the wall that divided those places—it was the merest sliver between them. I was far out of my depth. But now, from this vantage, I could almost see myself waking under the trees and riding the dawn train home, half asleep and full of longing. That truth was breathingly close again. It tugged and drew me back.

I still thought, somehow, that daytime life could go on as before. I stopped making the long train journeys. I knew the owner of the little bistro on the ground floor of our building, who had a storage annex she kept empty. I explained that I needed a dark place to retreat and meditate that wasn't far from home. The room had its own key and I don't think she ever realized how much time I spent there. I held on to my job for a while. Then savings lasted ed a matter of months, then I borrowed for a time from friends. During the days Easter and I lay in bed, watched TV, and had breakfast for lunch and lunch for dinner. Our little gaieties and struggles weren't much different than before, even with all I did and saw every night, but

I don't doubt that she felt something was different. Once, during the dramatic dialogues between her toys that occupied much of her time, she shouted,

"You are not listening to me! I will come and eat you!" She thought it was very funny when I dropped the folded towels and rushed to gather her up, murmuring into her hair.

Harrowers of hell, whatever form they take, are expected to free those who are worthy. If such a distinction could actually exist, I had no way of making it. I was not a creature designed for that. I was not meant to divine what laws subtended the other side, though I had surmised that going to hell exacted a toll of pain, and that escaping hell required something wholly contrary: mending, comforting, slicing the old ropes, forcing open the sprung trap.

More than any sense of duty or even compassion, it was simple base passion that made me return to hell to despoil it, joining the ranks of all the saviors and bodhisattvas, the knights and the harridans, the women and men (or former women and men), who had gone down to the shores of hell not to be lost but to retrieve the lost. But I believed that at least it was the passion of a great task of mending, so great it could be imagined only in fractions, in stitches and cross-stitches, through to the other side and across, and back through, and across, with my arms full of souls. Delivering, in an ecstasy of delivering, every night until I died, if I could die.

The babysitter arrived every night around Easter's bedtime, dropping his sleeping bag on the couch. I went four flights down, turned the corner, unlocked a heavy door, and closed it upon pitch darkness. I carried countless souls to refuge, striding through the walls between worlds. Sometimes they writhed out of my embrace and tried to stumble away, wailing when I caught them. Afterward, when they met their real bodies, they smiled at me, and sometimes wept for me.

I was a different thing than I had been, in ways not fully beyond my control. The winged demons were always present, if more cautious than before. I reserved all my pent-up wrath for them. When they came after us, I tore them to pieces. Often I cackled and howled. My laughter drove its taproot into the deeps from which this place springs and into which it flows.

I'm not sure how much longer I could have continued like that. I never found out, because finally one night, I couldn't go home. The dark storage room, abiding in the small hours of a Monday morning in spring, tugged me on its tether. Soon the babysitter would stir in his sleep on the sofa and try to phone me. But something had changed. The nameless faculty I had possessed, which had let me follow that tether back, was gone. I was furious, gnashing, helpless, racing in circles. What would dare? To bar me from where Easter slept, with her knees tucked under her and her face buried in the pillow? But I could only continue carrying over the immaterial bodies one by one or three by three, and pause to try again, and fail, and wait, and snarl and rage, and fail again.

Gradually, I understood—and maybe all of us, suffering bodies and fiends alike, understood it. Something had withdrawn from the worlds. Some upholding ground had not crumbled, but drawn back, and left everything to fall into the foundations. Some obscure negligence far above had taken catastrophic proportions below; some minor transgression below had raised great storms above. It could easily have been my fault. Or it was something humanity had done without knowing, or despite knowing, accidentally-on-purpose, bringing everything down with it. What had happened to me was a side effect of this calamity. Or was its cause. Or both were true.

Already the people were coming. Wherever they would otherwise have gone, here is where they all came, and the black-red earth couldn't hold them. Wave upon wave struggled and kicked to the teeming surface, bewildered and blind. The demons came flapping dutifully down but even they were taken aback by the great multitude of the newly dead. None of this should have happened, but now it was the end. Perhaps not the end of all things, but the end of many, many things.

When Easter used to drop a full glass of juice or trip over my laptop cord, I would calm her and myself by sing-songing, "these things happen." I let those chiming words carry me as I toiled—these things happen. All would be well with us, I knew, when we were together again. I began to see people I knew. I saw my daughter's father, spat up from the soil by the force of all the desperate others beneath, lying face up in blank pain. I carried him to the place of strange, tall grass under a muted sky, where he rose and walked. He didn't know me, but he cried for me. And after that, I did nothing but search for Easter.

Time failed. It spun like a toothless flywheel. I don't know how long I looked for her, digging down into the caustic earth while all the others suffered, unaware I had abandoned them. Over and over I clawed my way back up, wings ragged and freighted with dirt. Time spun and sputtered—and then I found her.

I lifted Easter and held her curled up on my chest, her head under my chin. The instant after we crossed over together, I wasn't holding her anymore. She was standing before me, staring and serious. Then her attention shifted: the world beckoned, just as before. She gazed all around, and began humming and singing to herself in little snatches and fragments, as she always had when she was happy. She stroked the grass and peered into it, looking for living, moving things.

"Mah-mee-mee…" were the syllables I thought I heard her chant, just as she turned and marched carefully away, in search of me or something else. I almost followed her.

Everyone came. It took time—just shy of forever and evermore—but in my arms and on my back I carried every single one of them over. This hell is empty now, as far as I can tell, except for the demons, who have nothing now to occupy them except me, and so soon they will be gone too. If there are other hells, I don't know how to get there, or how to leave this one anymore. If that thin place I entered and left so many times had any claim to be called heaven, I can't enter it again without someone to carry, to hold close. If I could, I believe I could not stay.

I have lived in this body now for time out of mind. It consumes, transforms, and expels nothing. It takes nothing in and ushers nothing back into the world. I think there is nothing it would not survive. If anyone or anything ever comes to retrieve me, they will find me in it.

Here I lie, in a hut I built of the bones of my enemies. Somewhere far from this darkened plain, beyond my ken, the last true battle has long ended. I try to remember my old, freckled, stretch-marked body, whose uses and wherefores are lost forever—my dark secret kept from no one, my irrational and consoling fantasy. I lie and dream about it, drifting as an anchorless bark into fog.

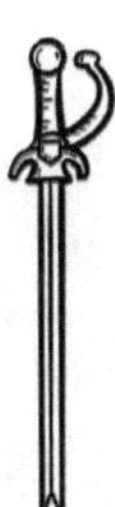

Just Me

~ *Ro Smith*

Dandrata ophosa meyrata mahan.

His earliest memory. Playing at the bottom of the long garden, near the ditch and the running stream and the strange sense of standing on the bank as though teetering but not falling—

not even close

—but hanging suspended in connection because . . .

Dandrata ophosa meyrata mahan.

Her mother in the kitchen kneading dough to make bread. And she doesn't even know what kind of bread, only that it will be warm and earthy—fresh from the oven, crisp enough to cut on the crust, but fluffy inside. This is seeds and milk-pounded-to-butter that was grass-for-the-cow, and they're not so very different really, but separate they are one-thing-here and another-thing-there, and together they are food and sustenance and people grow from them and people live and die and become food for worms and it's beautiful...

But she tells her mother that the bread will make her worm-food and her mother is appalled.

Sends her to her room to sit in the dark until she can
THINK
before
she
SPEAKS
But all she learns from the darkness is to be alone and
cut off from the bread and the grass and the cows and
the grain.

Until a spider brushes her hand and she feels the fly it
sucked dry and the ripe warm tomato where the fly laid
its eggs and—

Of course when she tells her mother about that it's
worse again.

But she hears it in the rhythm of the dough-pounding:
Dandrata

    The chewing of the cow:
ophosa

    The laying of the eggs:
meyrata

    The brush of the spider:

                                     mahan.

He's twelve and his father said he must invite boys to his
party and there are some and they're fine. They don't really know him, but they're fine.

He wants to play tag in the garden, but they're too old
now.

And he wants to play tag because what he really wants

is to play pretend that they are nymphs and sprites and dance in the muddy ditch and say it's a sacred stream—but when they were young enough to pretend they would have asked to play tag instead and he would have agreed.

So instead they play *man hunt.*

And one of them is hiding in the little wilderness beyond the ditch.

And he should be hunting that other—the other boys are laughing and shushing each other—but instead he hesitates at the old stream and feels a pull in its sluggish waters.

Dandrata ophosa meyrata mahan!
And the laughter bubbles out of him.

And he's like the other boys, but also not. Because this is beautiful—this rushing and hiding and brushing with branches and rustling in leaves and hands pressed down into soft loam and—

The forest is with them, but they don't even know.

And after he laughs, he sighs.

He knows where the hiding boy is, and he walks to him, holding out his hand.

The boy groans, but accepts it.

He is caught.

Those are the rules.

The rules they follow to do something that isn't about hunting men at all.

It's about running and hiding and rustling in leaves and burying your fingers in loam.

☉

She's an adult when her father dies.

They haven't spoken in years.

He wanted her to be a boy (who played with boys) and she wasn't.

And if not a boy, then a girl (who made bread with mother). But she wasn't that either.

Really, Dad just wanted *normal.*

And after all this time, with the funny moments and the words in the breeze and the lost minutes staring at water as it swirls down the drain . . .

. . . after all this time, she doesn't feel *abnormal.*

She's just whatever she is.

And so were the boys.

And so were the girls.

And so was the ditch that thought it was a stream and the bushes that thought they were a forest and the grain and the butter that thought they were the same . .

They all just were whatever they were, whether it was what Dad wanted or not.

And she . . . she had been far away from him for . . . oh, a time that floated on twilight.

Five years. She supposes it's been five years.

And then she hears it.

MAHAN!

A cry in the darkness across her cheese pasty as she fumbles for a grip on the rubber rail of an escalator.

MAHAN.

And she knows he's dead.

And she knows she has traveled a very long way to find herself so close to home.

At his mother's door he dies a little at the bell-chime call of familiarity in a depressed off-white button.

His mother's tears have stained her cheeks red, although they are dry.

"I keep hearing these words," he confesses, over the luke-warm tea they have both failed to drink. "I heard one and I knew. Before you called. I knew."

She looks at him, but he can't read the look.

"'*Mahan*,'" he says. "I heard the word '*mahan*.' And I've never known what it meant. But I've always known what it means. That's stupid, isn't it? That's what he'd say—I'm being stupid again." He ran a finger around the rim of his teacup, waiting for her sigh and correction.

"Not stupid," she says. "Just not what he wanted to hear."

He snorts, but doesn't look up.

"*Dandrata ophosa meyrata mahan . . .*" she says quietly.

Their eyes meet.

"'The tendril, the part of, all over, of us,'" she said. "That's what it means. You've always heard it, haven't you?"

"I . . . what?" he said. "That's nonsense."

"Did you hear it by the stream? In the trees?" she asked. "That's where I met him, you know. When we were young. And he asked me. He said: *Dandrata ophosa meyrata mahan*, and it meant that he wanted to be with me, not as man and wife, but as the stream and the trees and the mud and the forest. But I didn't understand. Human beings, we don't think like that. I said, if you'd be with me, you must be my man, and we must wed, that's how my people do it."

She frowned and brushed the hair from her face. "So he was. He was my man and we were wed. And for me, he was one of us. He wanted that for you. And you loved me too, so we thought . . . but you're still a part of that larger thing. Aren't you?

"I think what you heard—*mahan*—I think that was them calling him back. In as much as there is a him and a them. And maybe one day you'll be 'of us' again. You hear the call, but . . ."

"No, Mum," I interrupt. "I'm just me. I think that's what father never understood. I'm not them. I'm not us. I'm not a man. I'm not a woman. I am. And that's everything and it's me, too."

She looks away and I know she hasn't heard me.

"And he's everything, and so are you," I add.

She looks up and meets my eyes. Does she understand?

"Perhaps," she says. "Let's make some more tea."

QUEEN OF PENTACLES

Bloodletting

~ *Vera Hadzic*

After my husband's funeral, I went home and took my own blood, just as I had every Sunday for the past three years. The funeral had been dismal. I'd stood there, draped in black satin and gauze, like I was made of wax —like each passing second melted another inch of my flesh. The heat was heavy as lead, and humid. Just as his coffin thumped into his grave, the clouds had split open. His family had grumbled. They weren't used to Louisiana's afternoon thunderstorms. But I was grateful for the rain, even though it made me melt faster.

"You did the right thing," Michael, my husband's friend, had told me at the reception. "Keeping his body here. His home."

By now, I was so used to drawing my own blood that I could have found a vein with my eyes closed. The needle pinched as I slid it under my skin. The thin, plastic tube slithered down my arm. As it filled with blood, I felt it sigh. The bag swelled red. Through the window, the storm's breath gathered under my ears. The hulking, twisted oak on the edge of our property sucked the rain into its dark wood.

The day after the funeral, Michael visited. He brought another of my husband's friends, someone whose name I couldn't hear. I heard only the rushing of blood in my ears.

I took them to the living room. Made them something —tea, or lemonade, or coffee. I wasn't sure which. My gaze stuck on Michael's face, in its creases and its curves like sap. Today, he seemed so much more alive than my husband had been, but I could see the coldness in him—the pallor of his cheeks, the gauntness under his eye. My husband had, on his worst days, seemed a sheet of paper: like if you shone a flashlight on his forehead, you'd see into his skull.

"Was it really a car crash?" said the second man. "He was getting enough—you know? And it was good?"

"You can speak plainly here," Michael said. "We're all— friends."

Still, he looked out the window, at the oak tree as though its leaves were ears. As though the sunlight fermenting on the window could listen. Or as though the woodpeckers on the lawn wore wires.

"No." I was firm. I eyed my cup. Something brown— tea. Or coffee, with cream.

"But, if the source was contaminated—"

"It wasn't," I said. I put my right hand over my forearm, where the Band-Aid from yesterday kissed my skin. "He crashed into a tree. Branch went straight through his heart."

A week after the funeral, I took my blood again. A woodpecker ducked its head under the open window. Its feathered gladiator's crest was the same color as the plastic snake crawling over my arm. The bird tilted its head: *Where are you going to put it?*

My husband and I had met in New Orleans. The sun gave him headaches, so he slept all day in a dusky hotel room, blinds drawn tight. I'd had insomnia. At night, New Orleans glittered like a cracked kaleidoscope. The balconies' ironwork laced with light and color. Music, even. The stones vibrating under our feet had a heartbeat. Funny that a city's heart could beat louder than his.

I hadn't felt warm, or sexy, the first time he bit me. It hadn't even happened in bed. He had carefully laid his fingers over my neck, had felt for the veins. When I replayed the moment, I always imagined an open window, whispers of blues music bubbling into our hotel room. But when his teeth broke my skin, it was something like getting a flu shot.

In our bedroom, we'd turn on all the lights. Two weeks after the funeral, the room was still cluttered with the lamps we'd bought. We had chosen the yellowest, the orangest and warmest lamps. We had a ritual, racing upstairs, twisting each knob or button, watching the lights meld into a web of gold. We pretended we were in the sun, pretended it was the sun leaking into the pores of his skin, lighting up the shadows in his eyes. He'd hold me in his arms and tell me he loved seeing me with the sun braided through my hair. I was floating, he said. The second week after the funeral, when I climbed into bed after taking my blood, I left the lights off. It seemed wrong to enjoy our false sun without him.

Three weeks after the funeral, I heard from my husband's family. I was standing in front of the fridge when the phone rang.

"Fine," I told his mother. "I'm doing okay."

"That's good to hear." Her teeth worried her lip. "Would you like someone to come and be with you?"

She was relieved when I turned her down. I let her talk about how sorry she was while I rearranged the tiny glass bottles in the fridge doors. Whenever I moved one, the blood inside swirled into a red vortex. I poured today's blood bag into another bottle, stoppered it gently, put it in the place of the Tabasco sauce. I was running out of space. The peaches Michael sometimes brought me had rotted. I'd left the bowl on the windowsill and watched the woodpeckers' beaks tear the browning flesh into strips.

When Michael came next, he found me under the oak tree. His wide-brimmed hat shielded his face from the sun. It was five weeks after the funeral. The tree's branches, thick and oiled with moss, arched low over the ground, wooden snakes. It was a tree of spaces, each branch a basket of sky. The sparse green leaves offered little shade.

"We used to have picnics out here," I told Michael. "After dusk."

"What about the bugs?"

"Hell," I said.

He laughed, handed me another plastic bag. The fruit strained against it. Under this oak tree, I had first offered to draw blood for my husband. Right then, he would have become as translucent and sickly as stars behind smog, if he could have become any paler. But this had been a clear night, and the oak had buckled under the weight of the starlight. He'd agreed.

By six weeks, I was leaving the house more and more often. I took walks in the woods that curled around the property, waved a stick in front of me to tear down the spiderwebs that fizzle across gray-barked branches. I went alone. Spoke little if I passed any neighbors. Michael said he was glad to see me getting better. If anything, I was desperate to get out of the house. I'd stopped sleeping in our bedroom with all its lamps.

On my walks, I watched the birds coast low over the bayou, their red bellies warped by the gray-green waters. Heat cushioned my armpits. If a summer thunderstorm caught me, as it often did, I imagined that the mud suctioned a piece of me away with each step. When I got home, I drew my blood. Struggled to find a place for it in the fridge.

Eventually, Michael figured it out. It was the eighth Sunday since the funeral. At this point, the sacks of blood I filled, emptied, and refilled had become my timekeepers. The hands of a clock, a clock I couldn't properly read.

Michael found me by the window, plastic tube whispering along my forearm. Didn't say a word as we watched the red dribble into the fleshy sack. The woodpeckers thundered at the oak tree. I pressed a pale pink Band-Aid to my forearm.

"Didn't know you did that for him," Michael said finally.

I didn't answer. Didn't know how.

"He put you up to it?"

I shook my head. Offered him tea—I was pretty sure he preferred it to coffee. For a second, I wondered if I should offer him the blood I had just drawn. Or one of the chilled vials, one of the countless tiny bottles swaying in the fridge. Most of them, especially the ones in the back—filled before the funeral, or even before the crash—had darkened with time, turned earth-red or even black.

Michael took the tea. Slowly, he said, "I thought you were doing better. But this . . . isn't healthy."

"I can't stop." I swirled my tea.

"Can't stop?" He tilted his head. The shadow of his hat dripped into the lines of his face. "Or can't let go?"

He wanted me to talk to someone. *A friend. Family. Therapist. Anyone,* he said as he left.

I started filling the freezer with vials. I had already cut down on food to make room in the fridge. Let the fruit that Michael brought me rot. Thrown out meat. I couldn't stop, but seeing all the vials infuriated me. They spat in my face when I opened the freezer. Reminders that there was no one to drink them all.

I took my longest walks on Sundays, after I'd poured fresh blood into vials. These walks were free from memories. What I'd cherished in the first weeks since the funeral, the warm, tingly thoughts of our meeting in New Orleans, of our hotel room, our bedroom with its fake suns, were now difficult. I stripped the memories to pieces as my stick tore down spiderwebs in the woods.

I was at my weakest after taking blood, but I relished the buzzing in my head, the way my limbs felt light and wasted in the sun. Sitting by the bank of the bayou, watching the woodpeckers skim its sun-eating surface, was a kind of peace. The bugs that took to my arms made me feel better. Someone, at least, was using the blood in my veins.

At ten weeks, I slept in the kitchen every night. Sometimes I never bothered to get out of the chair by the window, where I could see the oak tree and let the woodpeckers drum me to sleep. I dreamed of my husband. Of our midnight picnics, our made-up sunlight. The precision when he sought out my veins. The softness in his voice, its warmth and richness.

Sometimes, I dreamed of the funeral. In those dreams, I really did melt away like a wax candle, turned into a puddle by a scorching thunderstorm. His family's lips curled in distaste, disgust. My thick, viscous self saturated the soil, absorbed by the earth: I pooled into my husband's coffin. The steaming hot wax, all that was left of my body, was acid to his corpse. Despite my best efforts, he dissolved at my touch.

Michael no longer came alone. He always brought someone new for me to meet—people who had never met me or my husband before. Sometimes they were his relatives, people with sunny eyes and tender handshakes. Or friends who thought I should come spend a weekend with them in New Orleans. I always said no. But I started to drink more water, to speak in longer sentences. When I had trouble remembering if it was week twelve or week thirteen since the funeral, I realized Michael's plan was working.

The fridge had been threatening to burst from all the vials I'd stuffed in. There truly was no more space. But it was my dreams that finally pushed me to empty it. After my husband's body flaked into nothingness, it was just me in the coffin. A puddle of wax, I could hear the rain punching the ground, could hear his family's footsteps echo as they trudged to their cars. Then, silence. As I cooled, I re-formed. The coffin shrank around me—its walls resisted the push of my palms, stood fast against the beating of my feet. I wasn't dead. I screamed I wasn't dead.

My husband's dead, I said to the coffin. *Not me.*

But the earth had swallowed me up.

When I woke, it was the first Sunday since the funeral that I didn't take my blood. I piled the vials into cardboard boxes, loaded them into the back of my car. Trundled up the sun-beat, dead-beat road to my favorite curve in the bayou, where I usually sat with mosquitoes and watched the red-bellied woodpeckers. I was tempted to throw each box into the water, to watch the vials sink. Instead, I opened them up, uncorked each bottle, and spilled its dark, shining liquid into the bayou.

It must have taken me hours, but I didn't feel the time. I heard my own pulse as thick red liquid clouded the water, bent into itself in sleepy, heavy curls. Soon, the bayou started sounding like my husband's voice. Viscous and slow, he said, *I love you, I love you, I love you.* He said, *I'm coming back.* He said, *Wait for me.*

Hours and hours must have passed because the sun had softened to molten orange, clinging to the tops of trees like globules of juice. And the water—I wondered if I was hallucinating. The slow current inched quietly along, all of it blood-red. All of it. As red as the plastic tube that meandered so often down my forearm. As red as an artery in my own neck. I couldn't look away.

The woodpeckers spiraled down from the trees, perched on the lower branches that twisted above the water, or by the bank. Their beaks shone, golden scythes in the fading sun.

Down cut the scythes, into the red water. Again and again, drinking up the blood, my blood.

Some of them were red-feathered already—the others matched before long. They descended upon the bayou in droves. For the first time, I couldn't hear a single one pecking against the tree.

I drove home. My fingers left luminous, sweaty prints against the steering wheel. First, it was only a couple, fluttering in the darkening sky, flitting by my mirrors. By the time I pulled into our long, sandy driveway, the oak tree was groaning under their weight. They fell silent when I stepped out of the car. Not even their red-soaked feathers rustled as I ran inside.

I slept fitfully, curled up and tangled in my own limbs on the chair by the kitchen window, the chair where I sat every Sunday to draw my blood. When I lay in my husband's coffin, I heard his voice inside my head. Felt it trickle through my bloodstream. Mingle with the wax of my flesh.

Why have you stopped? he would ask. *Don't you know I need it?*

Awake, I was chilled with sweat. I wore it as a blanket, a film over my body. Colder than his touch had ever been.

As the night went on, the woodpeckers swarmed the oak tree, lined the windowsill. Their beaks clacked against the glass. Their talons clamored against the wood. Their feathers whispered in my husband's voice.

They were here for my blood. Didn't they have a right to it? I began to think they were some part of him, some leftover part of my husband that had peeled away from his body when he'd been impaled.

I couldn't force myself to cry. I could hardly force warmth into my fingers and toes as I limped to the door, threw myself onto the porch. The simultaneous beat of hundreds of wings made a cylinder of sound around me. They tussled for space on the railing, hooked their claws to the beams above my head, hopped boldly on the deck. My knees dug into the wooden boards. My arms were as contorted and gnarled and aged as the oak tree, the one in the edge of my vision. I felt I might burst from all the blood in me, all the blood straining against my skin, begging to go out. A single prick from one woodpecker's beak might split me open.

But in all that time, the night had bled away. That was the sun rising, crawling along the spines of the trees ahead, flooding the gaps between them. The sunrise ate up the grass like fire, pooled into my palms like wax, like honey, and held me tight. It was red, redder than blood, redder than the woodpeckers' bellies, redder than how I'd felt when I heard how my husband had died. I had a redness in me, too. A redness just as burning, just as powerful, just as alive. A redness that belonged to me. I wanted to keep it.

The birds didn't make a move, or a sound, as I stumbled to my feet and leaned against my doorway. I let the sun, the real one, wipe away the gray in my face.

I boxed up the lamps in my bedroom and left them in the attic. My memories of my husband still ached, and I still loved them. But the weeks gained meaning again. I donated the equipment I'd used for drawing blood.

Some days, I went for walks in the woods—alone, or with friends. Often, I had lunch with Michael. And some weekends, I went to town, or to New Orleans, and let the city unravel me as it had before. Let its streets beat in tandem with my own pulse. The woodpeckers would never be far behind. They would caper on the filigree balconies, or hammer at the trees when I passed underneath them. Sometimes, they flew overhead, circling. Waiting for something I wouldn't give.

Occasionally, I left peaches for them on the windowsill.

Occasionally, I watched the sun rise.

KING of WANDS

Planet Preservation and the Art of Zen

~ Jetse de Vries

—a quadripartite prelude—

—The crisis is big, my children, so big that the distinctions between reality and imagination, impression and expression, even between fantasy and science fiction are dissolving—

The stranger is a presence, an epiphenomenon, an emergent property yet his followers prefer to visualise this ephemeral quadrilaterality as a person, an androgynous icon in zazen, floating in mid-air.

—The four of you must bear witness to the upcoming shift, the change of mental seasons. Short-term blindness, incessant greed, false conservatism, and fear are the four hard truths we must face. You must go the East, the West, the North and the South—

Four young adults are listening intently to the Swami of the four new Vedas. Chika Wu from Chengdu, her unruly black hair all but covering her amber face and glasses; João Incanna from Lima, his wiry frame and auburn skin weathered from years of fishing; Grace M'Boku from the Limpopo floodplains, her stature a study in empathy, ebony, and elegance; and Saaki Sami from Lapland, his springy red hair complementing his ivory face.

—Sow the seeds of change. Implement the memes of co-operation & entrepreneurship, innovation, long-term thinking & sustainability, and hope. Remember the four-fold path—the four new Vedas, if you like—to dharma:

- *the only constant in the chain of life is change;*
- *the protection of the weakest is the new way forward;*
- *like biodiversity, multiple strategies need not be mutually exclusive;*
- *greatness determines a people's karma, so find a way to improve yours;—*

Off they go. Wu to the East, Incanna to the West, M'Boku to the South, Sami to the North.

—a quadruple overture: four hard truths—

Chika Wu comes down in Chengdu, Sichuan Province, perched right between the Sichuan Basin and the fertile lands of the Chengdu Plain, a transit area from the Longmen and Qionglai mountains, the Min River convergence area and the extremely crowded cityscapes. The extremely polluted cityscapes.

Like Incanna, M'Boku and Sami, she has to form a team, a team that must focus on one big problem, a hard truth. The hard truth in China's cityscapes is impossible to miss. Pollution, eye-watering pollution everywhere. Breathing masks are as popular as smartphones, and more indispensable.

People are plentiful, perhaps too plentiful. Finding the right people might take too long. Yet almost everybody is connected to the internet in one way or another, with profiles, interests and surfing behavior readily available to those who know how to mine all that data. Wu dives in, searching for the right people, knowing that Chengdu is already a research & development center for new energies.

João Incanna remigrates to Lima. In the fishing villages of his youth, an immense hard truth is staring them right in the face. Through a combination of overfishing, pollution and climate change, the Pacific Ocean—the largest body of water on the planet—is slowly dying. Coral reefs are bleaching, fish stock are heavily depleted, huge amounts of plastic—in particular the plastic broken down to small pieces—are disturbing the food chain, biodiversity is suffering, and the acidity of the water is rising.

Compared to that, the poverty and lack of job prospects of the Peruvian coastal communities seem like minor problems. Yet Incanna wants to gather a team that aims to solve it all, step by step, little by little.

Grace M'Boku moves to Gaborone, then to the agricultural communities in the floodplains of the Limpopo River. There are many hard truths in her part of the world, but the hardest are hunger, disease, and destitution. Over the last few centuries, her people have been introduced—often forcefully—to new ways. So far, these new ways have mainly helped the already rich and well-to-do, and failed to improve the lives of the most destitute ones, like her community.

Returning to the old ways is not an option. There must be better new ways, ways like the waves of a tide that lifts all boats. Even if they have to invent those themselves, even if it means they have to work harder than ever before.

Saaki Sami shifts down in Luleå. Over there, the winter often covers nasty problems under a blanket of snow. But the winters aren't as long and severe as they used to be, and the blanket of snow is getting thinner by the year.

On top of that, some of the Scandinavians feel guilt about being a part of the problem. Companies like Ericsson and Nokia helped launch the mobile phone revolution, and the billions of discarded phones form garbage patches and landfills the size of small provinces. They helped deplete the Earth of many of its rare metals. It's time to clean up the mess and re-use those precious metals.

—circle the quadrangle—

Chika Wu's team is a weird mix of biochemists whose interests are restless, leaping from topic to topic like magpies chasing anything that glimmers; and physicists whose interests are so singular they almost forget there exists a world outside of it.

Both researchers wish to create their own Shang-tu, while also trying to improve upon already existing products and results. The biochemists wish to develop a thin, organic polymer film that acts like a solar cell. A film that's easy to produce, from materials that are widely available. A film that has a higher efficiency than the current best solar cell technology, and that is as maintenance-free as possible.

The physicists want to develop a room-temperature superconductor. Not only that, the material should ideally consist of parts that are readily available. On top of that, a material that can easily be produced as very long strands of wire, to stretch from mountain- or countryside (or desert) to city.

As she doesn't want the two teams to be fully isolated, Chika Wu hires an amount of interdisciplinary people who shift between the two core teams in an effort to provide both with fresh insights and ideas. The exchange proves so fruitful that a small group splits off from the other two and starts developing a new type of battery with record-breaking levels of power storage density.

João Incanna has introduced the fishermen of his port to a mixed group of University researchers, start-up entrepreneurs, and idealists. While the practicality of the fishermen often clashes with the lofty goals of the idealists, and the can-do spirit of the entrepreneurs often raises doubts with the researchers, a common goal binds them. They wish to clean up and reseed the Pacific Ocean so that its biodiversity can recover—and the starkly depleted fish stock with them—and deliver raw materials to the space-elevator-to-be base floating several hundred kilometers west of the Galapagos Islands.

So they work on a bio-active mega-net. An anti-fishing net of sorts, as it tries to catch the plastic floating around in the Pacific while leaving life—plankton, nekton and fishes—alone. To counter the acidification of the ocean they seed it with novo-plankton, a rich mix of genetically engineered algae, diatoms and protozoans provided with single-celled, alkali-producing algae. The algae will only produce alkali if the seawater's pH rises above seven.

The first prototype of the megabionet has plastic-detecting sensors that err on the side of caution, to be certain no actual living organisms are caught by accident. It lowers their effective catch ratio, but there is so much plastic in the ocean that it's better to launch the first vessels with the original megabionets than waiting and doing nothing. Later generations will be supplied with improved versions.

The first vessels with anti-fishing nets set out on carefully calculated trajectories, from the Peruvian coast to the North and South Pacific Garbage Patches—invisible from space, yet rife with plastic mini-, micro-, and nano-particles—and onwards to deliver the captured plastic to the base of the space-elevator-to-be, west of the Galapagos Archipelago.

☉

Grace M'Boku moves to Gaborone, where she goes after fresh University graduates, innovators young and old, and those willing to put in hard labour. In the agricultural communities outside the capital she looks for experienced hands and those well in the know about ages-old cultivation methods.

Her team—her 'agricultural advancers'—a mix of experienced and young people, needs to be wise enough to know what's right, then brave enough to choose it. They dance to the beat of the old world man with the heat of the new world woman. They have to be sharp enough to win the world, and wily enough not to lose it. Above all, as they try to move forward, they need to keep their nature pure.

Grace M'Boku's agricultural advancers must first face five years of hardship. Near the floodplains of the Limpopo River, the land is all but barren, and grand new techniques, together with ceaseless toil, can make it fertile. They must make agrichar and biochar—taking the best from chitemene—use new ways of mound cultivation to make the land, square meter by square meter, fertile again.

Not only that. After the land is fertilized, a careful mix of produce must be planted to maintain not only the fecundity, but the re-implemented diversity, as well. Beyond that, they have to make sure that the super-symbiotic neo-agricultures they've developed are also drought-resistant. Otherwise, one single super dry season will undo all their hard work.

She needs initial investments and—like other women, who form ninety percent of all successful applications—gets a microcredit for her project. She fully intends to be among the ninety-five percent who actually pay their loan back. After which she wants to uplift others in her region.

Saaki Sami gathers people from Finland, Norway, Sweden and Russia—with a few stray Icelanders—to form his research & development team. Reining them in like reindeer, he lures them with the carrot-and-stick approach of old guilt and new challenges.

His team is making something huge that incorporates immensely small parts. Not as big as an iron ore smelter, nor as large as Oulu's paper manufacturing plant, but still very substantial. Small enough to be easily constructed in other places, but large enough to take on big loads.

In their premises overlooking the snow-covered plains of the Scandinavian Arctic Circle, they're developing a high-temperature nano lubricant-cum-dissolver, a grey goo that's extremely resistant to high temperatures, able to penetrate the smallest of chips and circuit boards, with the ability to extract the rare metal needle in the discarded computing equipment haystack. Billions upon billions of computers, smartphones, tablets and other gadgets have been made, used and discarded in quick succession as Moore's Law ran its course. Enormous, polluting landfills where precious metals lay inert as current ores are running out. At some point intricate, intensive recycling will become economically viable. Saaki Sami's team wishes to be ahead of that very curve.

—the eightfold path—

Chika Wu's test project in Chengdu succeeds beyond her team's wildest dreams. Large panels covered with the solar nanofilm cover many square kilometers of the mountain- and countryside near Chengdu, and are interconnected with the cuprate superconducting wires. These same superconducting wires have been laid all the way to Chengdu, supplying the city with over ninety percent of its required energy. A coup emphasizing the solar nanofilm's efficiency considering the mostly grey weather of the area.

They also developed a more powerful type of battery. These batteries, implemented both in electric cars and houses have become plentiful enough to store the peak electricity production at day in order to keep supplying everybody with electrical power at night.

The test project is so successful that the Chinese government wants to implement it at a much larger scale in the Gobi Desert, to supply solar power to Beijing, Shanghai, and other megacities. Private entrepreneurs are already looking to implement the technology in cities outside China like Tokyo, Seoul, Bangkok, and Taipei, among many others.

Five years after the successful test project, the Chengdu Jintang coal power station has been shut down. Chengdu has now the best air quality of any municipality with more than a million people in China, and proudly calls itself the 'green revolution city'.

After the first five years, João Incanna's fleet is expanding rapidly. Simultaneously, the novoplankton-growing basins of his team are popping up everywhere along the Peruvian coast, even expanding into Chile and Ecuador.

The good they've been doing is surfacing gradually. Fish stocks are, slowly yet inevitably, picking up from their all-time lows. The novoplankton is thriving, both re-invigorating the food chain from the bottom up and countering the acidification of the ocean. Coral bleaching has come to a standstill, and a few coral reefs are steadily recovering. The plastic pollution levels are decreasing, albeit at a rate slower than they wish. His team keeps working hard to improve the efficiency of their megabionets.

The plastic they deliver to the space-elevator-to-be base is fully recycled into graphene and several organic by-products. The graphene is shot into orbit through a double railgun. The first railgun shoots up magnetized ice, most of which (flash-)evaporates in the atmosphere. Right behind it, in the magnetized ice's slipstream, is the real payload that does not burn up in the air. There, in geosynchronous orbit, is where the quadruple-redundant ribbon of the space elevator is produced.

Over time, they gather more plastic than is needed for the manufacture of the space elevator's ribbon, and they deliver the surplus to plastic recycling plants in North and South America. Big oil companies are either slowly dying out, or adapting, modifying their refineries into plastic recycling facilities. Crude oil production dwindles as renewable energy starts providing the majority of the world's energy needs and increasingly intricate recycling methods become competitive alternatives to crude oil's refined products. Slowly, for the first time in two hundred years, CO2-levels in the atmosphere are falling.

In Botswana, five years of toiling are followed by five years of feeding the people, modifying both their re-charring methods and their neo-agricultures to different types of lands and climates. In the original implementation areas—the floodplains of the Limpopo River—hunger became a thing of the past, and people slowly became better off as they were producing more than they could eat, and subsequently found willing markets for their inherently sustainable food.

The hard labour required to set up such a neo-agriculture provides much needed work. Increasingly, people aren't complaining that they're working so hard, but that they're proud to do such good work for the future of their family, friends, community and—in the long run—for their country and continent.

Their knowledge is made open source, but it doesn't spread as fast as Grace M'Boku and her people like, even as it's made available on every smartphone in Africa. Language remains a huge barrier, and they set up a quick translation app—at first manned by many human translators, more automated as machine learning catches on—that's sponsored by voluntary donations through moola from Mxit and other forms of electronic money. As their livelihoods increase, people are increasingly willing to pay their dues.

As a fortunate by-effect, sub-Saharan Africa starts to develop infrastructures old and new that need less original investments and maintenance such as vacuum Zeppelins for long distance transport, electric quads for short distance transport, and Electrified Trees for data signal transport, all increasingly powered by renewable energy. Their economies are growing in a highly sustainable manner.

After a series of increased fine-tunings, the prototype MaNa—Macro/Nano—Smelter in Luleå achieves recycling efficiencies of over ninety-nine percent, while being energetically self-sustainable and carbon neutral. The refined blueprint, which has been open source from the beginning, remains available to all. Siblings of the Lapland MaNaSmelter are popping up everywhere, world-wide. In a mere five years, the production of the newest device is truly green, sustainable, and fair. Fairphone in Amsterdam declare themselves obsolete and start a new project called

'Fairspace'. Landfills are rewilded after their soil has been purified by modified versions of the MaNaSmelters. Most of the mines are closed, their premises re-purified if possible, and rewilded, as well (even if a few are refurbished as appartements nouveaux). Eco-diversity is recovering, previously thought extinct species tentatively make a return, and Mercury and other heavy metal accumulation in the top of the food chain is diminishing.

On good days, the MaNaSmelter produces a small surplus of energy. Part of it is fed back into the grid, yet part of it is used for the sauna set up by Saaki Sami's team. After cleaning their minds and refreshing their bodies in the cleansing steam bath, Sami's people roll around in the snow, sky-clad and earth-bound. Is it psychosomatic, or are the winters slowly becoming colder?

—a coda of four kōans—

—If the strength of a chain is determined by its weakest link, how can the chain of life stretch endlessly long?—

—If the survival of the fittest was the grand design behind Darwinian evolution, what's the strategy in the Anthropocene?—

—How is the karma of a people determined? How can you strengthen your own karma?—

—Is it wise to explore another environment while you do not fully understand your own? Is it wise to remain in your own environment forever?—

Wayfinding

~ *A. P. Howell*

Becca didn't realize she always avoided part of the plaza until a sunny Wednesday when she noticed a weed growing in a cracked paving stone. She was very familiar with the paving stone and made a habit of looking down at it, stepping carefully on the familiar unevenness, taking special care during winter when pooled water iced over.

She stopped walking, feeling the afternoon traffic move around her. The plaza was big enough, uncrowded enough, that one non-moving body didn't cause any inconvenience. People simply stepped around her.

But not just anywhere. Becca wracked her brain to think of the different paths she'd used to get to class or the library or a food truck. Human memory wasn't perfect—the brain played all kinds of tricks, dumped useless data, and freely interpolated—but even allowing for that, Becca knew she had favored paths and there were certain areas she couldn't remember traversing at all.

She watched the other pedestrians for a while, uncomfortably aware that they also seemed to be avoiding some of those same spots. In the spirit of more scientific inquiry, she sat in a metal chair at an unoccupied table and watched for another hour.

A physicist friend had enjoyed making fun of the "unnatural sciences," and certainly anything involving human behavior was messier than optical equations. But her observations were still data, and in all the time she watched, Becca never saw anyone set foot in a five-foot-square area she herself unconsciously avoided.

Becca had a knock-off GoPro and zero desire to ask for permission to record or conduct any remotely official sort of study. She wasn't planning to keep the footage or publish anything. She was just curious, and an hour's worth of data was insufficient.

So she used a bit of duct tape to set the camera up in one of the potted trees bushes that dotted the plaza. She didn't have an angle on the entire plaza, but she had the Spot, as she had come to think of it over the past few hours. And even if focusing on the Spot made this an even less scientific endeavor . . . well, she wasn't aiming for publication.

Just one person, Becca told herself when she retrieved the camera the next day. Just one person stepping in the Spot would prove that there wasn't anything interesting going on, that she'd just observed traffic patterns and found, well, patterns. The human brain did that, but it didn't mean that any given pattern was important, or that it existed anywhere outside of that brain.

Except the pattern did exist, at least for the length of the video. Everyone avoided the Spot. Becca wondered if she had, somehow, missed something obvious. A broken bottle, a smear of dog shit, something mundane that her subconscious—that everyone's subconscious—had logged as a hazard to be avoided, but not so major as to attract attention. The video, however, showed nothing.

She looked the next day, too, and sat outside with a book open and unread in favor of people watching. No one stepped in the Spot.

She very nearly strode over and crossed that area herself. There was no reason not to, no danger or inconvenience. All her senses agreed there was absolutely nothing special about that Spot.

Nothing except the fact that she, and everyone else, avoided it.

And now that she knew, she couldn't quite bring herself to venture into that space.

She was supposed to think about the present and the future, how to mitigate the challenges of the one to make a bridge to an improved version of the other. History mattered insofar as it was part of the initial conditions, encoded in memory, culture, and built environment, but it wasn't what she did.

Becca spent time doing history. She found maps, helpfully digitized records of insurers, overlays she could apply to the now. The middle class neighborhood, digested decades earlier, formed a ghostly outline above familiar university buildings and the plaza, a bird's eye view of the past imposed upon the present.

She had known about the old neighborhood, of course, and other ways the city she inhabited had shifted and twisted and writhed over the years. But it was one thing to know about an old neighborhood (an old neighborhood, an ousted nation: all places were graveyards of the past) and quite another to have an address and floorplan.

The Spot fell in the middle of one of the ghostly row homes. Becca had easy access to a host of newspapers and census records through 1940. She should have been working on a GIS visualization, but instead she decoded fin de siècle handwriting and OCR mishaps. Lack of clarity between sixes and eights meant it took longer than it should have to find what she was looking for, but once she saw it she knew it was the answer.

In 1905, Louise Bromley, sixteen or seventeen at the time, had died in the house that had once stood where the plaza—and the Spot—were now located.

Becca had gone mad once. That was how she thought of it now, a small but significant number of years removed from an experience that had nothing to do with a mental health diagnosis.

She had been an undergraduate, a riot of hormones powered by caffeine cocktails. And at some point—she could not even remember the inciting incident—it had occurred to her that she ought to be more open-minded. Why were the truths of the present more certain than those of the past? Science, after all, was a construct, just like her own conception of time.

The lines between alchemy and chemistry, astrology and astronomy; the competing logics of religions; death and divination—these all fascinated her and, for a time, it seemed utterly uncouth to play favorites in the matter of belief. If some things might be true, why not all?

She could not quite remember how long the madness had lasted—six months? Nine?—but in a sense it did not matter. There was before-Becca and after-Becca, who was in almost all ways identical to her progenitor. But the detour into madness had happened, as profound (or not) as if she had cut her hair, shaved it off, dyed it, or wrought some similar change: time-bounded but still extant in memory and, perhaps, photographs or other documentation.

Which was to say, Becca had spent some time persuaded of the existence of ghosts. Not in the paranormal studies sense—such evidence had been debunked to her satisfaction, even when mad—but in a more philosophical sense. The human mind was a marvel. So, for that matter, was any complex life form, existing courtesy of eons of evolution and chance beginnings as single-cell organisms. The idea that something might persist was, in its way, less ridiculous than the belief that all that complexity simply vanished at the arbitrary point of death.

The Spot sat at a tantalizing intersection of Becca's past and present, her madness and her sanity. She neglected more coursework, datasets that had previously called out to her like sirens lounging upon silicon substrates, and instead mulled over questions of architecture and pedestrian traffic patterns and death.

Louise Bromley was nearly as much a ghost in the historical record as (perhaps) in the plaza. Teenage girls existed as lines on the census, written in another's hand. By virtue of her father's relative prominence—he had been a well-regarded doctor—there were a few references in newspapers, but aside from the tragedy's impact on her family, Becca learned little about the girl herself. This was frustrating but not at all surprising.

She supplemented the specific with the general, reading secondary sources about the life a teenager like Louise would have known. But social history, American history, women's history . . . these were not her fields, and they were too vast to master overnight and on a whim.

For half a day, Becca convinced herself that her bizarre detour was over. She worked on the visualizations she was supposed to be working on. And then she began to think about death again, and not just Louise's. All the suicides, all the murders, all the accidents, all the cancer and heart disease and aneurysms and pneumonia.

Why Louise? What was special about one dead girl? (Beyond the fact that every human life was precious, etc., etc.) Why could Becca feel her presence (absence, whatever) over a century after her death? And not just Becca: everyone else who avoided the Spot.

It wasn't until she slept and woke again that she realized this was a close-minded framing. Becca knew about the Spot, but that was no reason to assume it was unique.

Becca walked the city streets. She had always found it a useful exercise, a way of providing human-scale context for aerial maps and architectural plans and anonymized datasets.

Brick pavers uneven, raised by a tree's roots. A pit bull mix raised a leg to urinate on the curb; by the time Becca reached the small puddle, a boxer had paused at the same spot, adding its own scent.

She imagined the view from above, a complex dance of living creatures. Living creatures and dead: after crossing the street, she realized she had not walked in a straight line. Had a pedestrian died there, and did the resonance of that event prompt her to alter her path? So much life, death, and unlife: to even consider just this moment in time was more than her brain could encompass.

She thought then of brains, of neurological connections. Of the boundless potential of babies, and the way their brains grew by the pruning of those connections, the infinite rendered finite. Potential sacrificed in favor of pragmatism and response to the environment as the babies grew into themselves. Damage prompting workarounds and new methods of neurological wayfinding. Functionality defined by absence.

When she had been mad before, Becca had felt uncertain and compelled to study and rationalize her thoughts, ultimately classifying them as mad. That was not the case now. She knew Louise, insofar as she could know a stranger, long dead and poorly documented. She did not know the pedestrian, or the identity of the person who had planted the tree, or the reason dogs chose that particular place to mark territory and challenge another's marking. But her knowledge was irrelevant and Becca took a deep, almost religious comfort from that certainty.

She found a convenient stoop and sat across from a honey locust, listened to the wind in the leaves, the babble of voices, the sounds of traffic and a displeased cat, and felt the city grow into itself.

IV

Obverse Reverse

~ *Forrest Aguirre*

The odds were clearly not in his favor.

50,346 square miles of England, approximately 2200 years of numismatic history, most of it buried underground, and what was planned to be a twelve-mile hike along the Monarch's Trail, all versus a lone, middle-aged American tourist hiking the hills in worn-out tennis shoes, reliant wholly on luck, trying to find a misplaced antique or, better yet, medieval coin somewhere in his path.

No, not wholly reliant on luck, though it might appear so to any of the trail's ghosts or amblers who might happen his way. He had no metal detector, just a sassafras walking stick to aid in digging up any currency he might find stuck in the dirt. But Dalton Lapine knew something about "proper mindset" in turning so called "luck" one's way. He had, this late in life, abandoned the faith in ESP he had as a child and his dalliances with Chaos Magick that were all the rage when he was in his twenties. Religion never interested him. But he knew that "proper mindset" could hedge an individual toward his desires in subtle ways that made, or at least seemed to make beneficial coincidence more likely. He had used this notion much to his advantage, he felt, to excel in job interviews, to make smart moves with his investments, to get himself into desired relationships, then out of undesired troubles that usually resulted from those relationships.

And now, as banal as the circumstances were, his mind was set to find a coin to add to his collection on this hike. He knew it would happen. It had to. He willed it.

But it hadn't happened yet. Eight miles out along the path, on a stretch that claimed to be a "ley line," according to a book he had read, he was walking on a small portion of paved road that passed by a rural estate—a short-cut lawn a few acres in size, punctuated by well-kept rose bushes leading up to a sizeable (though not ostentatiously so) two story house in a faux-colonial style combining the worst of English Victorian and South Indian architecture.

Ahead of Dalton, a man rode his mower to a stop as the American approached, eyes to the ground. The air was redolent of fresh-cut grass, humid, and on the hot end.

"Did you lose something?" the man on the mower called out, wiping sweat from his brow.

"Sorry?" Dalton said, lifting his eyes.

"It looks like you might have lost something," the man said, alighting from the machine. "Can I help you find it?"

Dalton watched the man as he approached. He was the sort of man whose large girth implied strength and power, rather than indolence. Beneath curly red-brown hair and behind a thick mustache was the face of a man in his mid-thirties, though his sun-burnt features—a large brow and a wide nose, most noticeably, might have added a few illusory years to the countenance. He was dressed in a dirty yellow tank top, ragged cargo shorts, and cheap flip-flops. His teeth were terrible.

"Oh no," Dalton laughed. "I wouldn't want to keep you from your work."

"This?" the man held his hands out to indicate the breadth of the massive lawn. "I'm just mowing because the government makes me do it or pay a fine."

"You, you own this property then?" Dalton tried to hide his surprise.

The man chuckled. "Yeah, it's mine, mate." He reached out and shook Dalton's hand. "Name's Kevin. Kevin Shrike."

"I'm Dalton Lapine."

"Well, Dalton, I can tell you're American by the accent."

Dalton nodded, smiled shyly. Not your typical brash American tourist, then.

"Then we really need to find whatever it is you've lost or you might get stuck on this side of the pond."

"Ah, well, I haven't really lost anything. Really."

"What were you looking for, then? You were pretty intent on the ground."

Dalton hedged, embarrassed, then finally said "coins".

"Coins!" Kevin said with a laugh. "Then you're a numismatist?"

Dalton was pleasantly surprised that the man even knew the word.

"I have a small collection . . . back home."

"Well then, this is truly your lucky day," Kevin said. "I'm a collector myself."

The pleasant sensation that occurs when one discovers a fellow hobbyist shivered through Dalton.

"Have you found anything so far?" Kevin asked. "Occasionally . . ." He let the word hang in the air, among the odor of fresh-cut grass.

"No, not yet. I guess it's sort of a silly notion, thinking I might find a coin, let alone something valuable, on a random hike."

"Nothing's random," Kevin said with surety. Then: "They can be found," he said with a wry smile. "Oh, I know they can. I know," he emphasized the last word.

Dalton, encourage, perked up a bit.

"I'll keep my eyes to the ground, then."

Kevin, staring hard at Dalton, as if assessing him, yet never dropping that mischievous smile, said "Perhaps you'd like to see some of what I've found?"

Dalton held his hand up in protest. "Oh, I couldn't impose. Besides, I'm keeping you from your tax duties."

Kevin looked at the grass with a sudden frown.

"This? This can wait. The tax man will always come and collect his dues, whether we want him to or not. Besides, you'll never come this way again."

Dalton considered, bobbing his head from side-to-side, as if weighing a decision.

"Never again," Kevin repeated. The smile returned. "Come on then, I insist."

☉

The inside of the house was more stately than Dalton had expected. Surely, he had misjudged Kevin's dress and accent. He wondered how such an ordinary-looking and, to all appearances "lower class" man had come upon such a posh estate. He never voiced his questions.

Kevin led Dalton through a portion of the manor, lemonades in hand, to a broad, sunlit room whose windows looked out over an immaculate rose garden. Birds and small animals flew, hopped, and crawled their way through, oblivious to the two men inside.

"Idyllic," Dalton commented.

"They know the place is safe for them," Kevin replied, taking a set of keys from his pocket. He set about unlocking a row of long, glass-topped tables, which held scores of coins in protective plastic sleeves. "I can't get away with having all this and living alone, without some measure of security."

"Wow," Dalton said in a reverent half-whisper, as if on sacred ground. "You found all of these?"

"Most. Not all. I bought maybe half a dozen to fill in gaps. One was given to me."

"Given? That's generous."

Kevin did not respond. He put his hand on his stomach and a pained look crossed his face. He gulped down his lemonade and stood still for a moment as the pain passed.

Dalton, gazing on the collection in wonderment, barely noticed.

"It looks like you went to the continent for some of these."

"Many times," Kevin said. "Germany, Austria, The Netherlands, France. Here," he pulled out a coin and handed it to Dalton, "this is a 1612 Seville 4 Reales that I found while snorkeling off Majorca."

After closely examining the coin, Dalton handed it back.

Leaning over the display cases, Dalton again scanned the collection.

"You've got a Thaler here I've never seen; 'JOHAN:-GEORGE.ET.AUGUST:FRAT.ET.DUCES.' Ah, Saxony. What year?"

"Go ahead and take it out. The date is on the obverse, but I love the reverse portrait so well that I keep it wrong-side up."

"1612," Dalton said after pulling and examining the coin. "Elector Christian II. I'm not familiar. I'll have to read up on him and the pair on the back."

"He was dead the year before that was minted. Nothing particularly spectacular about his reign. His brother, one of those on the reverse, though I can't remember which one, took over as Elector of Saxony. He was similarly un-impressive."

Dalton replaced the coin then, making his way to an-other table, he peered through the glass.

"What's this?" he said, pointing to the far back corner of the case.

Kevin had his hand on his stomach again and the furrow to his brow and squinting eyes indicated even more pain.

Dalton looked to his host, but did not mention the man's expression, not wanting to offend him.

Kevin forced the beginnings of a smile and nodded his head toward the coin, as if indicating to his newfound numismatic friend that he should examine it more closely.

Kevin nodded in the affirmative.

"Are you okay?" Dalton asked.

"I'm fine. Excuse me for a moment. I'll be right back. Feel free to take anything out to examine it, just please put it back in the place you found it."

"Of course."

Kevin passed through a pair of double doors that led into a hallway that was lined with bronze sconces. Dalton thought he caught a glimpse of a suit of armor as the door closed.

The coin that had caught his attention did so because of the dark patina that covered its face, quite unlike the other coins, which shone with gold or silver brilliance. Perhaps it was heavily-tarnished silver? The coins position, atop a small pile of Elizabeth I silver groats, might have indicated provenience, but there was no visible date on it. One side showed the ¾ portrait of a grim-faced, bearded man wearing a Burgundian sallet, partially obscured by a high pauldron. An arquebus rested on his shoulder. The lettering around the legend was worn down so as to be inscrutable. The other side of the coin (he assumed to be the reverse, though there was no clear indicator that the knight's portrait was the obverse) showed a crudely-fashioned image of a hare standing on its hind legs, with its forepaws upraised, as if engaged in a human dance. Above it, in the air to the left, was an image of the sun with a fine-featured human face on it. To the right was a similarly-visaged crescent moon.

He squinted hard, then, finding a lamp, turned it on and held the coin directly under the light. On the hare's side of the coin he could make out the phrase "+Lepus dolorum+," in the legend, but nothing else.

He found himself fascinated by the motif and mystified by the legend. He could only imagine the story behind why that phrase became engraved. Why would anyone label a coin "rabbit of sorrow"? He walked back to the case, determined to ask Kevin about the strange words and image.

But then, he thought as he walked back, what is stopping me from studying it out and learning for myself?

Butterflies erupted in his stomach as a thought, then a nervous desire, then utter cupidity arose in him. Kevin's words echoed in the memory halls of his skull: . . . *you'll never come this way again.*

Kevin returned to the room to find Dalton, hands respectfully held behind him, looking down at the case furthest from where he had left him.

"This 1748 Maria-Theresa-Taler," the American said, "is it a replica? Forgeries are so common on these."

"No, it's an original," Kevin said. "I've had it certified twice."

"It's in beautiful condition," Dalton said, turning to look at his host.

The man was pale as a ghost, but the smile had returned and any indication of pain was gone.

"You're doing better, I hope," Dalton said.

"Didn't drink enough water while mowing, is all. I got some in me and am feeling much better. Thank you for asking."

Dalton looked at his watch.

"This has been fabulous," he said, "but I must be moving on, soon. Dinner reservations and all that."

Kevin nodded. "Understood. You've travelled over an ocean to be here and taken a long hike on a hot day. You'll be famished by the time you get back."

"Mmm, yes. But before I go, would it be okay to take a few pictures of some of the coins?"

"Absolutely, Dalton. Be my guest," Kevin said.

"Oh, but I already am."

Dalton could not hide a smile.

The clothes in his suitcase were piled up like a volcano, slopes spilling out onto his bed, and at the bottom of the crater, nestled snuggly in fabric, the coin. Good, it had made it through security and across the ocean without an issue.

Dalton removed the coin, oblivious to the mess he had made. His usual fastidiousness was cast aside as he clawed the object out and unwrapped it.

For a brief second, he though that the coin had somehow been replaced by another, but that was ridiculous. Yet, something was different. He checked the legend: "+*Lepus dolorum*+" was exactly the same as he remembered it. Looking at the knight's portrait however, Dalton questioned if he had, in the excitement of the theft, falsely remembered the face of the knight being more hale, less gaunt than it now appeared. The eyes seemed to be shadowed in a way he couldn't recall, the beard slightly less sparse than he remembered; and the stern expression more attentive, as if the knight was coming into awareness about something that had been heretofore hidden.

Flipping the coin back over, he was startled to see that the rampant hare had moved from the position he remembered. And wasn't the moon closer to full now? Surely, the waxing was a function of the sunlight, which shone more direct at his latitude than it did at England's. That must be the explanation.

He found a lock box and, though he could hardly stand it, placed the coin inside and tucked the box in a drawer before preparing for work the next day. He fell into a deep, jet-lagged sleep.

The following day at work was long and grueling. Dalton had literally hundreds of E-mails to check through and his work was frequently interrupted by well-meaning co-workers asking about his trip. At first, he regaled them with detailed stories, but as the day wore on, the resolution of his recitations became more and more pix-ilated. The longer the day went, the more irritated he became. By the end of the day, he grew sullen, until he could check out and leave.

Once home, he retrieved the lock box and opened it. He stopped reaching for the coin when he saw the knight's face again. The eyes had sunken in and dark-ened, and the muscular upper-body (apparent even un-der the armor) seemed thinner. This definitely was not how the coin had looked the day before.

Looking at the reverse, he swore the hare had moved, drop-ping to all fours and appearing, like its obverse, to be thinner, the eyes darker. The moon, Dalton noticed, had grown again, nearly to a half-moon. The sun seemed smaller.

But he must have misjudged the images on the coin previously. He had no picture to compare against, as it had been in his pocket when he took pictures of the oth-ers. This time, he would record the coin as it was with a series of photos.

The second day of Dalton's return to work was less de-manding, but no less taxing. His energy would lessen with his interest in work, leaving him bored and tired. After lunch, he fell asleep at his desk, then startled awake with no idea of how long he had slept. He stood, yawned, and ambled to another co-worker's cubicle—Michael Schwent's—to talk about the upcoming football sea-son, as well as to answer Mike's many e-mailed questions about Dalton's trip to England. The conversation stretched for as long as they felt they could get away with it, then Dalton meandered about, taking the long way back to his desk where he fiddled with spreadsheets and meaningless tasks until quitting time. He didn't quite succeed in fully waking up until his shift ended, after which he felt a sudden rush of enthusiasm that kept him alert for the walk home.

The closer he got to home, the more the anticipation of seeing the coin again rose within him. He picked up his pace. By the time he got to his apartment door, he could hardly put his key in the lock because of the shaking of his hands.

Once inside, he pulled the coin from the place where he had secreted it, nearly dropping it, but catching it before it fell to the floor.

As he held it up to examine it, he wished that he had let it drop.

He didn't need to check his photos to verify the changes.

By the end of the work week, Dalton's boss had sent him home early. "Get some rest," he was told. "You really ought to see a doctor. You sure you didn't catch something while you were overseas?"

He visited the doctor, just so he could say he had, if for no other reason. He was hardly awake for the appointment, mumbled a few things automatically, feeling as if he was more and more outside of his own body. Sheer willpower kept him from collapsing, "proper mindset" . . .

A prescription was written.
Home.
A handful of pills.
A shot of whiskey.
Sweet oblivion.

Kevin was on his back, desperately trying to crab-walk away from the looming hedge in front of him. But his hands and feet continuously lost purchase in the slippery grass.

A shadow, darker than the gloomy, cloud-covered night, emerged from the hedge, shaking and rattling its branches, sending a shower of moisture onto Kevin's near-prone form. The etiolated shade was nearly as tall as the hedge itself. A pair of long ears, pulled by the tug of the hedge, trailed behind the head. Pinpoints of pure void, a black that one felt more than saw, projected loathsome rays from the place that might have been a face.

"I haven't got it!" the man on the ground cried out in a piteous, pleading voice. "I don't know where it went! If I did, I'd bury it in the burrow; you know I'd do that for you! But I don't know where it went, now do I? You can't hold me responsible if I don't know what happened to it. That wasn't part of the deal!"

Kevin's screams . . . no, his screeching, his mewling, begging, sobbing still echoed in Dalton's ears as he rolled off the couch and thumped on to the floor.

He got up off the floor and looked outside—sunrise on the eastern horizon. To the south, the full moon was half-hidden by the edge of the Earth. It was Monday. He set off to work.

Around six o'clock, Dalton found that he had caught up on all of his work and even worked through what was supposed to be a long-term project that he had begun in fits and starts before he had left for England. No one had disturbed him and no mention was made of his being sent home early the past Friday, though water-cooler gossip about the incident had surely made the rounds.

He noted that Mike was also around, working late on some machine-programming project for the shop floor, no doubt.

"Hey, Mike," Dalton said.

Mike looked up from his work, welcoming the break with a smile.

"Dalton! Glad you're back with us in the land of the living, man."

"Yeah. You heard about last week then?"

"Someone told Paul . . ."

"Then everyone knew," Dalton said with a half-disgusted smile. "Anything else happen while I was out?"

"Nobody told you?"

"About what?"

"Seriously? I can't believe no one told you! So, after you left last Friday, some dude comes in through the front door looking for you, asks for you by name."

"Weird."

"Not even the start of weird, my friend. Stephanie is kinda freaked out because this dude is cosplaying as a knight."

Dalton's smile fled.

"I kid you not: armor, sword, 'thou' and 'thy'—the whole schtick. Dude was super-hipster, with the twirly mustache and pointy beard. And he would not drop character! We could barely understand him, though he was trying to speak English."

Dalton stood gape-jawed and wide-eyed.

"Some euro-trash you met in bloody old England?"

"No, I . . . I don't know him. Look, I need to get back to work. Gotta stay late to make up for lost time."

"I hear ya. Anyway, glad you're back and in working order."

Dalton went back to his cubicle and stared at his monitor for a long time, numb. Mike left, calling out "good night!". Eventually, the night security guard told Dalton it was time to lock up.

"As they say at the bar: 'You don't have to go home,'" he joked, "'but you can't stay here!'"

Rain and the rumble of thunder had moved in by the time he left for home. He had left for work that morning in such high spirits that he had utterly failed to check the weather. The thin trill of cold water down his spine reminded him, now too late, that he should have brought an umbrella.

Overhead, cloud-smothered lightning occasionally gave a dull glow to his immediate surroundings, not quite compensating for the rain's damping of the already-inadequate streetlights. It was under that dull, irregularly-pulsating light, accompanied by low thunder, that revealed to him that he was walking past one of the larger city parks, a riverside strip thickly-crowded with willows and bushes, the municipality's attempt to extend the river bank's natural reach out into the city.

Amidst the burble of water and the groans of the storm, Dalton thought he could hear rustling among the trees. He stopped, momentarily preventing the tapping of his shoes on the road, and listened.

The rustling, as of animals in the bushes, sounded again, then stopped.

He moved on, shoes tapping, sometimes splashing in a puddle. The sound in the bushes continued.

He stopped.

The sounds in the bushes stopped.

He continued and, as he did, became aware that whatever was in the vegetation was matching his movement, stride for stride.

He walked faster.

Then ran.

Ahead of him, off the road, amongst the trees, he heard a familiar voice.

"That's him!"

"Kevin?"

"That's the one! There's your man!"

The clank of metal on metal sounded from the hedge. A large shadow emerged, shattering branches as it crashed out. Fallen sticks pinged off the armor.

Between the knight's feet, a hare stood upright, ears perked, nose twitching.

From behind the pair, as if from a great distance, he could hear Kevin's voice:

"Time to collect the debt, Dalton Lapine. The crown always gets its taxes. Always."

The hare shot out, sprinting full-speed toward him. He could only stare.

He heard the click of a hammer on a flash-pan, smelled gunpowder mixing with the scent of rain on the air and a flash blossomed out from the shadows. Thunder sounded.

He wasn't entirely certain if the thump of the striking bullet or the springing rabbit reached him first.

It was night again. His feet were cracked and bleeding from the long hike to get here. The rabbit flopped around inside his belly, kicking and pushing against his ribs so hard that he thought they might burst out from the skin.

He opened his hand and looked down at his palm, where the coin lay. He flipped it around. Dirt was still encrusted in the legend's divots, between the gothic-scripted letters. He mused on how far the dirt had travelled, how far he had travelled, since he had felt the compulsion to disinter the coin from the ground outside his apartment, where he had buried it.

The sun shone brightly above the wholly-restored hare, who leapt and danced on the meadow, the moon only a faint sliver.

The knight's face had transformed. It was now a more familiar face. His prominent brow, curly hair, and mustache were even more exaggerated on metal than in the flesh. His teeth were still terrible.

Closing his hand on the coin, Dalton looked at the estate, knowing the treasures that lay therein. He smiled, despite the pain the hare was giving, kicking him in the ribs. Kevin was right: the tax man always comes to collect his dues. Kevin was right about many things.

All, save one.

Dalton, clutching his distended belly, stumbled onto the lawn, toward the house.

He was here, again.

VII

Scorched Planet
School of the Arts
Course Catalog
Fall Semester 2120

~ Lorraine Schein

Degree Offered: B.A. (Bachelor of Apocalypse—Terminal Degree)
The goal of our school is to prepare students to be able to exchange their artwork for food or shelter in a dying eco-system. Upon graduation our students have found freelance work for private clients or jobs in the corporate death field.

All students must choose one required major concentration and two minor electives from the following:

DESIGN CONCENTRATION

Portfolio required and a score of 850 or above on the SAAAT (Scholastic Apocalyptic Arts Aptitude Test).

FASHION
Prereq: Design 1, Sewing Techniques, Microbiology
Students will design full hazmat suits that are flame-proof, virus-proof and have attached gas masks. Workshops cover creation of clothing that converts to a house, submersible boat or teepee.

Successful fashion major graduates have been commissioned to design face and body masks for private and corporate clients.

BODY ART
Prereq: Needle Techniques 1 & 2, Art History
Students will learn how to create and apply original designs using ink and laser techniques for applying tattoos on irises and construct migrating nanotattoos on a variety of bodies.

HABITAT
Prereq: Oceanography 1, Physics, Architecture 1, Materials 1, Shop Class
Prospective architects will design house pods with legs or flying houses that will avoid floods, expandable houses, and immersible submarine dwellings.

WEATHER CONCENTRATION
Prereq: Astronomy, Anemology, Chemistry, Meteorology, Flight School 1
NOTE: Students with a current pilot license are exempt from the Flight School requirement.

SKY ART
Prereq: Heliology, Color Theory 1
Students majoring in Sky Art will manipulate sunlight to create unique sunsets and sunrises that stay up all day or night and are moveable to any location. Graduates have found freelance work in both the private and corporate sectors.

RAINWATER ART
Open to Weather majors only by permission of Professor Roy G. Biv.

Prereq.: Color Theory 1, Meteorology, Psychology 1, Pluviology
This course will teach seeding of clouds with color-infused droplets to create varied shades such as iridescent and rainbow spectrum rainfall. Graduates have found employment in both the private and corporate sectors.

RAIN MUSIC

Prereq.: Harmony 1, Meteorology, Audiology, Pluviology, Roofology
Students will create original musical compositions using directed rainfall, orchestrating rainstorms and rainfall into musical compositions. Graduates have been commissioned to compose orchestral pieces for private and international clients.

RAIN SCENTING

Special Topic. Open only to students who have completed Rain Music and Rain Art and permission of advisor.
Prereq: Aromachology, Osmology, Neuroscience.
Students will learn to create scented rainfall.

CLOUD SCULPTURE

Advanced Seminar Prereq.: Art History 1, Nephology, Portfolio Review
Learn techniques for carving cirrus and cumulus into portraits and landscapes.

DISASTER ART CONCENTRATION

Our graduate Disaster Artists have found employment with regional warlords, career military, and major corporations. Eligibility Requirements: Open to students with a criminal record and/or a portfolio evidencing psychopathology and interview by a former advisor on probation from Arkham Asylum.

WILDFIRE ART
Prereq.: Pyrology 1, Printmaking, Explosives 1, Flight School 1, Pyrotechnics 1 and 2 (Preference given to students with high SAAAT scores on pyromania.)
Wildfire students will design and selectively burn areas of forests to create aesthetically pleasing patterns using foam retardant and explosives dropped from a plane to form control lines.

HURRICANE PERFORMANCE ART (Independent Study)
Students must have an interview with department head Professor Marvel and obtain permission of instructor, staff psychiatrist, and next of kin.
Prereq: Photography, Videography, Sky Diving, Aerial Stunts and minimum 4.3 grade-point average in prior Weather courses.
Under faculty supervision, students will design, choreograph and write the script for a special interactive performance to be performed within a hurricane of their own creation. They will then photograph themselves inside it as well as document the wreckage below.

BLIZZARD PERFORMANCE ART (Honors Project)
This advanced course is only open to surviving Hurricane students with a grade-point of average of 3.5 or above and permission of advisor.
Prereq.: Cross-Country Skiing, Snowboarding, History of Antarctica
See Hurricane Performance Art above for course description, but colder and snowy.

POLLUTION ART

Prereq.: Oceanography, Intro to Questionable Business Practices, Urban Nonplanning

Students will learn to create a variety of artistic pollution such as smog, particulate matter, and nonrecyclable plastics. They will measure and document the effects of environmental degradation on animal and human health in their chosen environments using such indicators as exceeding the Air Quality Index standards, the creation of plastic islands in the sea and rates of coral death.

DEATH CONCENTRATION

Prereq.: Biology, Abnormal Psychology, Morbidity 2, and permission of Professor H. Lecter.

DEATH DRAWING STUDIO

Prereq.: Art History, Anatomy 2, Taxidermy 1, Decomposition 1 & 2, Forensics Pathology

Students will draw portraits from expiring models and photographs of extinct and endangered species.
Formaldehyde tolerance test required.

DEATH LITERATURE (Work/Study)

Prereq: English 2.6 (Shakespeare's Tragedies), Japanese Literature, Gravestones 1, Journalism, Videography, Snuff Cinematology 1

Students will learn to create and write deathbed poems and narratives for dying and suicidal people and document their deaths by posting on the web, Facebook and TikTok. Graduates have been hired by gang lords and employed by major political parties.

VIRUS ARTS

Prereq: Virology, Biology, Genetics 1 & 2, Pathology, History of Germ Warfare, Culinary Contamination Skills

Students will learn to design and infect populations with new viruses using recombinant DNA and devise their possible cures. Fall Semester: Designing Viruses. Spring Semester: Reverse Engineering for Antidote Vaccines

QUARANTINE TECH

Prereq.: Virus Arts, Information Technology, Network Administration, Sexology

Students will explore advanced 5 Senses Zoom techniques such as Lurid Imaging with Realtouch™ peripherals that allow online self-pleasuring or group orgasms. Topics covered include the synchronization of lucid dreams to simulate the experience of pre-pandemic socializing.

BODY DEFORMATION

Prereq.: Genetics 1 & 2, Anatomy, Biology, Mutation Surgery, Abnormal Psychiatry, German History 2

Using directed mutilation techniques and plastic surgery, students self-sculpt and sculpt others to create malformed designer bodies. Techniques studied may include cloning, Botox augmentation, abdominal fat redirection, feather transplants. Includes off-campus field trips to mental hospitals and prisons to select subjects for operations and visiting guest lecturers from the Moreau Institute of Body Hybridity. Successful graduates have found work in the entertainment industry and for international clients.

Fog Net

~ *Sarah Day*

Oleg stole my fucking ICCA grant.

Okay, he didn't steal it. That's not accurate. He was awarded my fucking ICCA grant.

Okay, it wasn't my fucking ICCA grant.

But it *would* have been mine, if not for Oleg.

I'm the best grad student in the department. First author on three papers. Four patents. Senior editor of that stupid journal only a dozen people read. I haven't been on vacation in two years. Sasha's always saying he never sees me anymore. And why? Because I'm the best grad student in the department. Everyone says I'm headed for the Oceanology Institute. Everyone says I'll be a full RAS member before I'm thirty.

Unless fucking Oleg puts a shiv in my career by taking my fucking ICCA grant!

And to do what? Burn some reindeer shit? They want to give a boatful of money to someone studying REIN-DEER SHIT?!

Okay, Vika, calming breath. Do that synapse breathing you heard about in that podcast. This isn't good for your blood pressure.

List the things you still need to do today:

- Email Vitaly about re-running the neohydrolysis test with those new meteorain magnets. Space magnets = more H20 faster?
- Get to the bug peddler *before* 7pm today—the line's been awful since no one can afford quadruped anymore and the hen flu wiped out all the poultry.
- Buy a pregnancy test. Stress is one thing, but three months is maybe too long.

. . .

. . .

. . .

It's because alternative energy is sexy right now, is why. Everyone wants to be the one to outrun the oil shortages. Failing that, they want to be the ones who funded the person who outruns the oil shortages. So here comes Oleg with some barely-plausible idea about waste reconstitution, can't they see he's just reinventing the omni-processor? The Gates Foundation already did this, but he went on about how Russia has the best chance to develop the biofuel that saves us because of the unique environmental factors in the taiga and the grant committee just dropped to their knees. Their *knees*. Over *reindeer shit*.

I suppose if I'm going to be completely honest, his research position does paint a slightly more hopeful picture of the future (tldr: we can maintain our current population and living standards if we're all willing to smell burning reindeer shit every time we go outdoors) than mine does (tldr: we're fucked into the seventh generation, and we should accept it and get moving, because

our septly-fucked descendents are going to need *water*).
I get why that's attractive. But still.

I am medicated to prevent me from feeling feelings
EXACTLY LIKE THIS.

OLEG!

☉

Dear journal,

Another day, another dollar. Or another thirty thousand
dollars because (surprise!) it turns out the seawall still isn't
fixed. Almost a quarter-mile of wall gave way overnight.
Found one of the condensers on Jake Willet's front lawn. It's
okay—neohydrolysis gel is pretty durable (thanks Mom!).
With no rain in four months and the sea advancing on us
like the indecisive hand of God, losing a condenser would
be a disaster. We're already timing our showers.

Speaking of water, the high school gym is sunk in two
feet of it, thanks to the wall breach. I went down there
this morning. Smelled like fish shit and feet.

I thought Mox would be freaked out, but nope. Stood
there watching the ocean eat the only school in town,
like "At least the greenhouse is dry, we can still save the
sprouts." Remarkably chill little person I have there. No
idea where that came from. Not me, that's for certain. I
just had to up my blood pressure meds.

I *told* Public Infra putting a second layer of concrete
on top of the first layer of concrete would just make the
wall erode faster. But why would they listen to me? I'm

just the mayor. Just the person they elected based on the strength of my environmental agenda, my fresh ideas. Just the son of Dr. Viktoriya Aleksandrova, Russia's Nobel-prize winning climate oceanologist, the woman who invented neohydrolysis. My name's on the darn doorplate, right? IVAN ALEXANDER. Sheesh.

And I have fresh ideas! They just take humanpower, which we have, and money, which we don't, and time, which we're running out of.

No one wants to abandon the coastlines, reestablish the topsoil with trees that can tolerate more water (cypress, zelkova, I have a whole list!), pull away from the sea, regroup uphill. Everyone is so focused on maintaining what we have, they're not interested in what we could do.

There are the bad guys outside of town, too. That's what Mox calls them, but I shouldn't even write that down, probably. Some of them are technically my constituents, not that any of them are registered to vote.

~~Bad guys~~ Racists ~~Bad guys~~ Psychos ~~Bad guys~~ Christian death cultists

I'll just stick with bad guys.

I think people in town find them as abhorrent as I do and want to avoid moving inland. I hope that's true. I want it to be true—I want to be safe here as we were in Seattle. Constituency be damned, I can't shake the hand of a man with me-colored skin and a cross tattooed on his neck and then go home and confront Zara's eyes staring at me out of our kid's face. Our half-Black kid.

I miss her every day.

I can see the wall from here. My desk faces a window and on clear days I can see the fleet of condensers bobbing behind the upper lip of the concrete slab. At high tide, water slops over the top like beer over the rim of a glass.

Thank God hops have such high heat tolerance. We may be sinking like Atlantis, but at least we still have beer.

- I

○

Spring, 1 year after the fall

No idea how to keep an almanac.

No idea how to do anything.

Spring

No one knows what they're doing. Everyone would rather be back in town, but the flooding's so bad it's not safe anymore. The buildings are dissolving, except for the housing shells we moved the condensers into last year when the seas got too rough.

Everyone coming to me for suggestions on seedlings and planting schedules and square footage, like having a botany degree means I'm Mox Alexander, Farmer. Pff. I can't even keep an almanac right.

Still, you do what you can do. I might not be a farmer, but I can make a green thing grow.

Mox Alexander, Grower.

Spring

Planting season. Dog-ass tired every day. Hoping everything roots soon enough that it can survive the summer. It's early spring, but everything's gotta go in the ground as soon as it thaws.

I miss cheeseburgers.

Spring

Bad guys came to the farm today. They wanted our food. Enough of us here to warn them off with just numbers.

Elli wants to move us back into town, maybe see if we can fix up some of the old buildings. Something secure, she says, for winter, but I can tell it's not just that. I saw how the bad guys looked at me. This is a pretty pale population, and I stick out.

Spring

Cherry blossoms!

Summer, 1y ATF

Lost Patrick today. Tiller threw a rock, hit him in the face. Popped his eye. Total surprise. Patrick was our doctor. Kirsten's brother. Fuck.

I can hear Elli crying in the next room. Want to comfort her, but not sure what to say.

Not sure what to say.

Rock whipped him around in a circle like he was dancing, like the news he was dead had to catch up to the rest of his body.

Summer

Hop harvest. Condensers still working, thank God. Every couple days a crew goes into town, lets themselves into the shells, taps the condensers, and comes back with carts of fresh water. That and the catchments off the barn mean there's plenty of water to go around. Gonna make beer.

Miss Dad a lot.

Sept 21?

Sun calendar I keep on the kitchen floor says it's probably the equinox.

October 1ish

Elli's fixing up one of the housing shells in town. Lots of the panels are damaged or missing, but she's starting to repair them, put flexiplas sheeting over the holes. She says if we can scrounge enough material from the dead buildings in town, maybe we can build up a whole network of domes, use them as greenhouses, maybe get the solar working again, maybe live in them, maybe maybe maybe.

Madness. She's always got a big dream. I love her.

November???

Small group came to the farm. They looked rough. Hungry. Faces I thought I recognized—some of the bad guys from the spring? But there were little kids with them. Never imagined the bad guys having kids, but that feels stupid, writing it out. Of course they do.

Don't know what they'd come here for anyway. Barely enough for us to eat.

Winter, 1y ATF

Cold AF.

Winter

One of the condensers died this morning. Not sure if it's a problem with the fans, or with something electric in the box itself? Elli's as close as we have to an electrical engineer but she couldn't make the thing work.

We peeled the neohydro gel from inside the casing, at least. Might be we can add it to the gel in an existing condenser, or save it in case something goes wrong with another.

Fuck it, I'm tired of trying to solve problems.

Bad day.

Winter

Moved into the domes today. They're not all done, still a couple gaps in the upper panels, but the wind got too bad to stay on the farm. Trees going down everywhere. Was worried about the sprouting shed blowing over, taking all the seeds and cuttings with it. In here they'll be warmer, better protected.

Nice to be in a modern building again. The farmhouse leaked like a gassy husband.

Spring, 2y ATF

Planting season. Every day we trek out to the farm before dawn. Walking home in the evening, I can see the domes going up against the sky. Four already and more to come. Don't want Elli up on the ladders much longer—belly's getting too big. Kid should be here by midsummer.

Spring

Blight in the cherry orchard.

Spring

Bad guys came again. Smaller crew than last year, but meaner looking. Had to plead with Elli not to meet them at the farmstead with the rest of the crew. Length of rebar in her hands like she was gonna whack someone.

"It's my home too, Mox," she says, "I can fight."

She's my home, though, and the baby. I talked her out of it.

Spring

Losing the cherry trees a big blow; fruit, yeah, but also morale. No more branches floating on the breeze. No more blossom season. Feels like nothing good can last, sometimes, like we're unspooling the last of our thread.

Enough of that.

Summer

One of the condensers broke today. Down to three now. If we lose those, we're fucked, we'll have to move uphill and that's where the bad guys are and . . .

Be cool. Be cool.

Rainy season was good. Catchments are full. Gonna build a cistern. We can get through this. We've gotten through everything else.

Summer

Baby's coming.

☉

— Log start —

They arrived at dusk yesterday and camped outside the domes. Probably forty of them. I went up on the upper walkway and looked through the panels at their camp. Little fires. All the people dirty and scraggle-haired and stooped. They look so hungry.

Tersa went out to greet them and didn't come back. My baby.

She's so smart, nothing can have happened to her. Nothing has happened to her. I know it.

— Log start —

They want the condenser. One of them, a big man wearing armor made of old tires, came to the antedome today and said so, speaking through a two-inch slit Timor opened in the external door. They know we have a means of making fresh water. He said give it to them and they leave us in peace.

I don't know what they'll do if we tell them the condenser fell silent ten days ago and has yet to wake.

It's not exactly dead—water coalesces on the transparent fleshy lining inside the box, weeps down the walls like sap. You can press a cup to it and come away with enough to drink. But it won't suffice to quench the dozen of us inside the domes, much less the people clustered outside.

Still no sign of Tersa.

— Log start —

They'd like to get in. The doors are holding.

I understand why they'd want to. I remember how the domes looked the last time I was under the open sky. Like soap bubbles full of treasure. The plant dome looks like a green jewel from the outside, and the solar cells gleam in the daylight. It's clear we have power in here, real power like they did in the Old Times . . . although nothing so fine as then. Even with all the cells running, harvesting the light, we have to ration. No one under fifty is even allowed to touch the terminals, leave logs like this one. Guess they figure that's how us old folks can still contribute, ha ha, by sharing our memories.

Did Momma and Moxda plan for this, when they rebuilt the domes? That we could use them not only as a resource, but as a refuge? They must have. The plant dome, sleeping domes, the gathering dome—they're only connected to each other, not to the outside. You have to go through the vestibule dome to get into the world, and all the ground-level panels are reinforced with metal and concrete. We could shelter in here for a very long time.

— Log start —

The condenser continues to sleep. Its six twisters should be running together, giving off the quiet hum that became the background to everything in the plant dome. Aurel says the box was powered by a phantom, and now it's escaped. I think Aurel is a superstitious idiot, but I haven't a better explanation than that.

— Log start —

I saw Tersa! She clambered up the panels and peeked in through the flexiglass. She looked annoyed, but she always does. I wish I could crack the exterior door and let her slip back in, but until those strangers outside are gone, she'll have to make do outdoors. She's clever. She'll be all right.

I spent extra time at the sprouting altar, talking to the seedlings and thanking the earth for its providence. My heart. To see my daughter alive, I, I can't describe it.

– Log start –

They're trying something new today. They've felled a tree and are trying to ram it into the exterior door. When I hold my breath, I can hear the muffled thuds against the metal.

I wish the condenser was working. Maybe if we could give them some water, they would go away.

– Log start –

They took Timor. He wanted to speak with them, the stupid child, and as soon as he had the antedome door cracked an inch, they had branches and spears wedged in, trying to pry it open. They seized him and pulled him out, and two of their own slipped in.

I was in the plant dome when I heard the commotion, and by the time I got to the pressure door, Aurel had sealed it, and used the control panel to lock all the other doors. The two outsiders are trapped in the antedome now, prowling like wildcats. They're holding spears, faces swabbed with mud. They look angry.

They look hungry.

I don't know what happened to Timor. I think Horvel does, but from his face I don't want to ask.

— Log start —

The outsiders changed their approach overnight. They sent a dozen young people up onto the smaller domes, so when we awoke bodies were stretched across the panels like spiders. Even as I speak they're trying to prise up the capstones, peel away the roof panels.

Aurel and Brillia took the little ones out of the school dome and into the plant dome, just to be safe. They said it was because the strangers' shadows were distracting, but I can tell they're worried.

Fortunately the bigger domes are too round to climb easily. Now we're all clustered together in the plant, sleeping, and gathering domes. Even if the strangers can make it into the little domes, the pressure doors should keep us safe. Eventually they'll give up, go away.

— Log start —

I went up on the observation walk this morning and saw the outsiders have erected some kind of structure outside the doors. It's like a T with an extra growth on top, or an X tipped on one point. There was a group gathered around it, one of them standing in front of it waving his arms. I couldn't hear anything, but they looked like they were chanting, or singing.

I don't understand anything anymore.

— Log start —

They destroyed the storage dome today. Idiots took too many panels out of the top, and it came down almost atop them. I think one of them got trapped beneath.

We've never lost a dome before. At least it was one of the small ones. If the outsiders go away, perhaps we can rebuild it.

If they go away.

I hate them.

— Log start —

In my dream last night, the domes cracked open like eggs. We all tumbled out in a spurt of saltwater and stale air, each coated in a gel skin like the inside of the condenser. I was bloody and wet and I rolled over on the ground, trying to identify my limbs. That sleeping state where you know you have a body but don't know how it's composed. I flopped onto my belly and worked my mouth, searching for air. I looked up and saw Tersa standing at the waterline, bright clean and new.

Momma told me that that's how people came to the Earth, that long ago we arrived on the shore as fish.

— Log start —

They're at the pressure door.

☉

". . .What are—? Holy crap. You're kidding. What are you doing here?

"Who would leave a baby out in the dirt? Guess they thought they were coming back, didn't they. Idiots. Pulled the whole dome down on top of them. And on top of my people too. Obviously. No survivors . . . Present company excepted."

". . . Fuck. Okay. Come on, Tersa. Breathe. Stop crying."

. . .

"I can't just leave you here, can I?

"At least you fit in my backpack."

. . .

"They killed my family. Our seeds. Everything. I'm alone now—except for you, I guess. You're basically a seedling yourself. A person-sprout.

"I wonder what your name was.

"I'll tell you one thing, sprout, we're gonna have plenty of fresh water. Those idiots—your people, sorry, no disrespect—they broke all the way into the domes, killed Timor, killed my family, didn't even know what they were looking for.

"Aurel thought the condenser was some kind of magical house, that a baby god or something lived inside it, but Aurel's—fuck, Aurel *was* a loony.

"It's not the box. It's the *gel*, the snot coating the inside of the box. It sucks water out of the air, somehow. So once the haze cleared from the collapse, I went in, found the condenser. Lucky I got there when I did—the sea's hungry to eat what remains of the domes. Got the box open, scraped out the gel, found a jar to put it in. Like a big blue loogie. Gross, right? But it still works—see? I take the lid off and it makes a little puddle on top!

"Nonono, don't touch it! Don't—ugh."

. . .

"Okay sprout, how's about we get away from the coast? There's probably more food inland. I don't know about you, but I don't want to live on seagulls and shellfish. If I could catch any seagulls. Or find any shellfish.

"Anyway, I figure we head east and see what's on the other side of the mountains. You in?

". . .You're in."

. . .

"Hang on. Hold still. Let me get this tarp around you. Dust storms aren't gonna be great for your tiny eyes. Hold still. Hold still. Shhhhh. There we go."

. . .

"You like that? That's rabbit. Thinking it over? Hah! Great face.

"Good, right? Here's another little shred. Get that in you, help you grow up real big.

"Glad you're old enough to have real food. No idea what I would have done with an infant."

. . .

"Ohfuckohfuckohfuckohfuck are you okay? I'm so sorry. I'm *so* sorry. I would never drop you on purpose. I just slipped. I'm so sorry. Fuck. Are you okay?

". . .I think you're okay."

. . .

"Ughhhh you're *heavy*. We're only halfway there. I'm hoping that the world is greener on the other side of this hill, because summer's coming out here and I don't know about you, but I'm tired of the dust.

"*Bigass* hill. Basically a mountain."

. . .

"PLEASE STOP CRYING."

. . .

"Wowwww. Look at that view! Not as green as it could be, I guess, but it's still awfully pretty. All those rock formations! Wish I knew anything about rocks!

". . .All this natural wonder is lost on you, isn't it, kid? Jeez.

". . .Wait, what is that? Do you see that?"

. . .

"Okay, so what did we learn? There's people down there. People with what I guess are probably guns. Never seen a gun before. One of them took a potshot at us, I dunno if you noticed that. Thanks to my quick thinking, I fell on my ass, so hopefully they think they got me. Fuck, who shoots at a single person up on a hill? Why do they have those red tattoos?

"Oh. Oh *no*. Oh *fuck*. They broke the fucking condenser jar! Or I did, I guess, when I fell on it! You okay? No glass on you, right?

"Uggggh, this is a disaster, how the fuck am I supposed to carry a gallon of mostly-liquid gel without a container? There's goo all over the inside of my pack! UGH.

"Okay Tersa. Silver lining. Silver lining. At least they

didn't hit *you*. And the jar's somewhat intact. It'll still work for a little while, I'll just have to be careful not to cut myself.

"And also? In those rock structures on the other side of the valley? I think I saw the land in rows, like they were planting. Plumes of smoke. Maybe a town."

. . .

"Okay sprout, I've got this idea. Aurel told me that back in the Old Times, people used to catch water with nets, really fine-woven fabric on frames that would wick the condensation out of the air. Fog nets.

"Honestly I think it might be made up, but it's also kinda how the condenser goo works. If we stretch it over something, we can produce more water; if there's regular airflow over it, even more. We gotta carry it somehow, we might as well carry it on us. At least it's sticky.

"See, what I'm thinking is, if we can make it to that village, they might let us in, keep us safe from those red-tattoo people, if I had something to trade. Fresh water's a pretty good thing to trade. So we spread the goo over ourselves like a big blanket, our own fog net, and show up on their doorstep just absolutely dripping. Impressive, right? What do you think? Sprout?

". . .Are you falling asleep?"

. . .

"Okay, first things first. We gotta get around the valley basin. I got most of the goo back in what's left of the jar, and I'm thinking as soon as the sun starts coming up, we head out around the southern edge of the valley."

. . .

"Look, sprout. We were right—it's a village. Wow, it's built *into* the side of that big rock formation. How did they do that? That's nuts. Oop—watch your step. Watch my step, I guess. Slippery. Goodbye, rock. Jeez that made a lot of noise. Yikes."

. . .

"Hsssss okay. Oh fuck. Oh no. Fuck that hurts. Fuck.

"You okay sprout? Please be okay.

"They shot my fucking arm!

"Okay Tersa. Deep breath. Get moving. Your feet aren't broken. Just your arm. My arm . . .

"Stop crying! Move it!"

. . .

"I know, I know, it's cold. I'd cry too if I was you. Let's get this goo over us. Man, we smell bad, don't we? Been out here for awhile. I'm shaky. Not long now, though. Not far. Just another couple hundred feet. We can make it.

"Yikes, that *is* cold. Okay. You ready? It's you and me, sprout. You and me all the way."

. . .

"HELLO! Hello in there!

"Sprout, shh. Someone's coming out."

"What—who's out there? What are you wearing?"

"Please let us in. We have water. I'm hurt. We need help."

". . .Who are you?"

"I'm Tersa. Tersa Adlar. And this is Sprout."

☉

A DL E
AD LA R
ADLAR
Sprout Adlar
Lucee teach me how to write.
My name is Sprout Adlar.
Lucee ses says write abot war because I was there. I don't have all the words to write abot war.

We won but we lost. The redsky people took some of us, our dead. That's their way. But we keep the ones of them we ~~capch~~ captured. And we keep the fog net, which is why they came here to start.

Happy Tersa didn't have to see our dead go with them in the wagons. She would cry a lot.

I miss Tersa.

Better at war than words.

Tomorrow they will come again and we will talk. Maybe there will be no more war. Maybe we give their captured for our dead. Maybe a lot of things.

☉

Today I raised the fog net and my people's hands bore it.

There's no predicting the rainy season anymore; some years, spring is just a handmaiden for a dry, blazing, tower-cloud summer. Others, the winter skulks off like a coyote, with rain the sound of the brush closing behind its tail.

I am the cloudwatcher, and I declare the harvest, so when the darkness crackled over the west horizon I summoned the eight attendants and carried the fog net to the circle altar atop the mesa.

When the bottom fell out of the clouds, sixteen hands pulled the fleshy membrane wide, until it was thin as a whisper and jittering with the impact of raindrops. I darted beneath the net and lifted the point of my staff.

Rain hit the sloping net and multiplied itself as it ran. Far more water than the clouds provided sobbed off the edges of the net and into the basins set beneath the altar. Each basin drains into the tile-lined cisterns we've hollowed out of the mesa's stone heart. When full, they can sustain us for months.

This is the blessing of the fog net, to give as much water as we're strong enough to hold.

Standing underneath, I watched the net marble. Faint shadows sluiced down my limbs, the ghosts of rainwater. The scent of the storm rioted in my nose; ozone, wet dust, the sweet exhalations of desert plants opening to receive the rain. The net began to weigh heavy. I shoved the staff up against it, working the muscles in my back and shoulders.

Lightning fluttered across the bruised sky. Beneath the altar, the basins glugged and laughed. Being under the fog net was like returning to the womb; dark, stifled, more sound than sight. The world outside the net melted into a blur of grays and blues, the attendants hovering just beyond like eight midwives, ushering in the future of the mesa.

Two of my spouses were among those holding the net. I watched their fingers twist tightly as the weight of water belled it out. Water ran in sloppy sheets off the edges, splashing around their feet. The other six attendants come from the mesa villages. Three of them bore the red-inked knuckles and nails of the Red Sky tribes, who until a generation ago had been our enemies. Perhaps we would be at war still, had my father, the first cloudwatcher, not brought members of the Red Sky atop the mesa, inviting them to hold the net and share the harvest with us. I have reason to be grateful for that—the first Red Sky woman to take up the net later became my mother.

The air inside the net dimmed as the rain thickened. I shouted to hold fast, hoping to be heard over the roar. Water cascaded off the net in such abundance I could no longer see the attendants' feet. I wondered if this would be the time someone's hand slipped, or the net tore, or there was some other catastrophe—but my spouses were strong, and the other six were strong, and the net held. In my heart I felt we could hold until the bottomless cisterns filled, until the pipes backed up and the top of the mesa was ankle-deep in the womb waters of the fog net.

My father says that when he was small, the fog net made water from the air passing over it, that a child's breath could render its blue-silver skin damp like the underside of a stone in the early morning. I don't know if that was ever true, or if he's telling me a fable, trying to keep my idea of magic in the world alive, trying to keep my heart hopeful, like a child's.

He doesn't understand that I don't need hope.

All things are temporary. I know the net may fail. I know my people did not spring up here on the mesa but arrived, and that someday we may depart. I know death swallows each of us.

But not today.

I am Anat, daughter of Sprout, son of Tersa, daughter of Steff, daughter of Mox, child of Ivan, son of Viktoriya, and today I raised the fog net and my people's hands bore it.

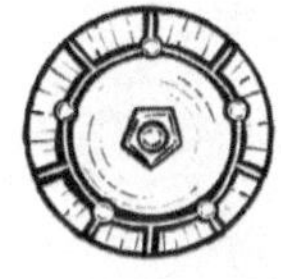

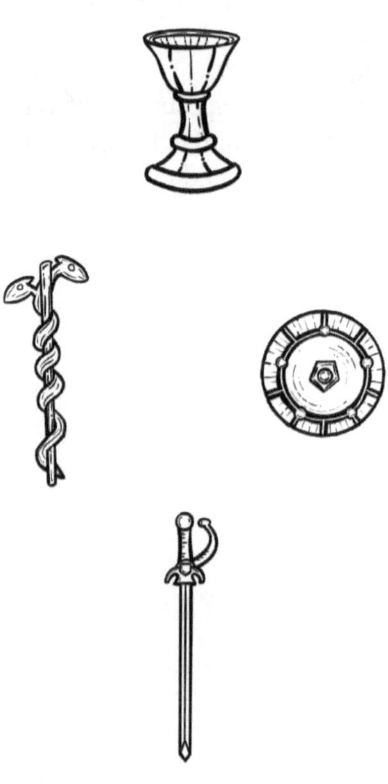

CONTRIBUTORS

Forrest Aguirre

Forrest Aguirre's work has appeared in over fifty venues, most recently *Vastarien*, *Infra-Noir*, and *Synth*. He has also written several roleplaying game supplements including *Beyond the Silver Scream* and *Killer of Giants*. He is a World Fantasy Award-recipient for his editorial work on the *Leviathan 3* anthology. His novel, *Heraclix and Pomp*, is available from Underland Press.

He hosts the blog "Forrest for The Trees" at forrestaguirre.blogspot.com and can be found on Twitter @ForrestAguirre.

Forrest lives in Madison, Wisconsin.

Brandon Crilly

An Ottawa teacher by day, Brandon Crilly has been previously published by *Daily Science Fiction*, *Abyss & Apex*, *PULP Literature*, *On Spec*, Flame Tree Publishing, and other markets. He received an Honorable Mention in the 2016 *Writer's Digest* Popular Fiction Awards, reviews fiction for BlackGate.com and serves as a Programming Lead for Can*Con in Ottawa. With Evan May, he's the co-host of the podcast *Broadcasts from the Wasteland*, described as "eavesdropping on a bunch of writers at the hotel bar."

You can find Brandon at brandoncrilly.wordpress.com or on Twitter: @B_Crilly.

Sarah Day

Sarah Day lives in the SF Bay Area with her cat and a large collection of LED lights. Her interests include creature films, festival culture, and doing things on purpose. You can find her at sarahday.org or on Twitter @scribblingfox.

Jetse de Vries

Jetse de Vries—@upbeatfuture—is a technical specialist for a propulsion company by day, and a science fiction reader, editor and writer by night. He's also an avid bicyclist, total solar eclipse chaser, single malt aficionado, Mexican food lover, metalhead and intelligent optimist.

On March 28th, 2021, he posted the world's first NFT SF novel on Ethereum's Mintable. The landing page on his website "The Future Upbeat" lists where his debut novel *Forever Curious* is available. https://www.the-future-upbeat.com/

Manfred Gabriel

Manfred Gabriel's short stories have appeared in over two dozen publications, most recently *Liquid Imagination*, James Gunn's *Ad Astra*, and *Crimson Streets*. He lives and writes in Western Wisconsin, where he spends his days dealing with people and writes at night to keep his sanity.

Vera Hadzic

Vera Hadzic is a writer from Ottawa, Ontario. Recently, her work has appeared in *Hexagon Magazine*, *Idle Ink*, *Okay Donkey Magazine*, and elsewhere.

She can be found on Twitter @HadzicVera or through her website, www.verahadzic.com.

Catherine Hansen

Catherine Hansen lives with her family and teaches literature in Tokyo. She grew up between rural South Carolina and urban Japan. A book with Strange Attractor Press, titled *In Search of the Third Bird*, represents—at the same time—her latest creative work and her latest scholarly work. One day, you may well find her on Twitter.

A. P. Howell

A. P. Howell lives with her spouse, kids, and dog, sometimes near a lake and always near trees. Her stories have appeared in *Daily Science Fiction*, *Little Blue Marble*, and *XVIII: Stories of Mischief & Mayhem*.

She tweets @APHowell and her website is aphowell.com.

Christi Nogle

Christi Nogle's fiction has appeared in over thirty-five publications including *PseudoPod*, *Vastarien*, and Flame Tree's *American Gothic* anthology. Christi teaches English at Boise State University and lives in Boise with her partner Jim and their gorgeous dogs.

Follow her at christinogle.com or on Twitter @christinogle.

Lorraine Schein

Lorraine Schein is a New York writer. Her work has appeared in *VICE Terraform, Strange Horizons, NewMyths,* and *Mermaids Monthly,* and in the anthology *Tragedy Queens: Stories Inspired by Lana del Rey & Sylvia Plath.*

The Futurist's Mistress, her poetry book, is available from Mayapple Press (www.mayapplepress.com).

Ro Smith

Ro Smith writes fantasy and science fiction that challenges our assumptions about reality through the veil of fiction. Ro has a doctorate in epistemology and metaphysics from the University of York and her short stories have been published by Distant Shore Publishing, Fox Spirit Books, and *Hub Magazine.* As an non-binary author it means a lot to her to represent a diversity of identities in her fiction.

You can find Ro on Twitter @Rhube.

PAMELA COLMAN SMITH

The tarot images in this issue of Arcana are from the deck illustrated by Pamela Colman Smith. It was released in 1909 as the Rider-Waite deck (so named, at that time, in reference to its publisher, William Rider & Son). It remains the most influential and widely used tarot deck. While the impetus for the deck came from Arthur Edward Waite, Colman Smith was responsible for the iconography of the cards.

Pamela Colman Smith also illustrated over twenty books, wrote two collections of Jamaican folklore, edited two magazines, and ran the Green Sheaf Press, a small press devoted to women writers. She continued to write and illustrate throughout her life.

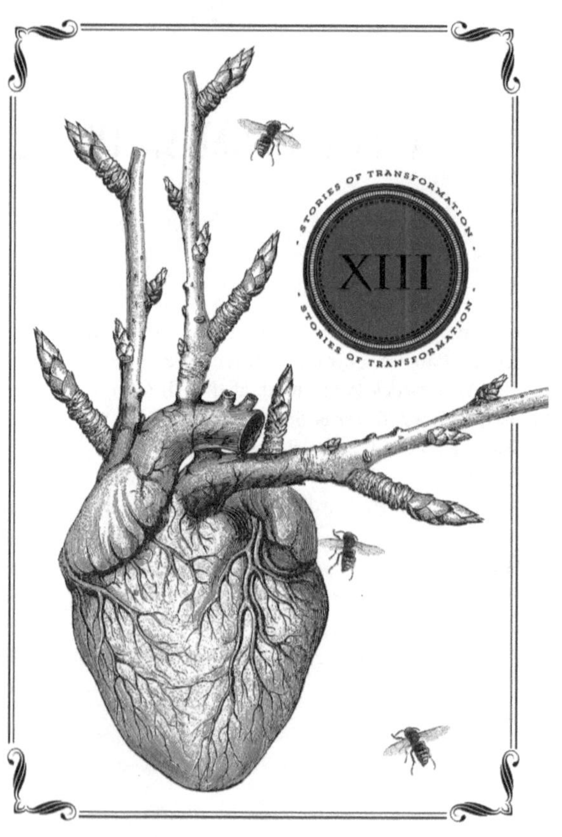
STORIES OF TRANSFORMATION
XIII
STORIES OF TRANSFORMATION

XIII

The thirteenth Tarot card is Death, and he is a symbol not of the end, but of transformation and rebirth. This is the genesis and root of *Thirteen: Stories of Transformation*. The twenty-eight authors of this collection are voices—new and old—who are not afraid to explore what comes next. Whether it be a life after death, a life without love, a life filled with hunger, or the life shared by a ghost. These are stories of the weird, the mythic, the fantastic, the futuristic, the supernatural, and the horrific.

With stories by Liz Argall • M. David Blake • Richard Bowes • George Cotronis • Amanda C. Davis • Julie C. Day • Jetse de Vries • Jennifer Giesbrecht • Daryl Gregory • Rik Hoskin • Rebecca Kuder • Claude Lalumière • Marc Levinthal • Grá Linnaea • Alex Dally MacFarlane • Juli Mallett • Lyn McConchie • Fiona Moore • Gregory L. Norris • Adrienne J. Odasso • Cat Rambo • Andrew Penn Romine • David Tallerman • Tais Teng Richard Thomas • Fran Wilde • A. C. Wise • Christie Yant

Edited by Mark Teppo.

Available at independent bookstores everywhere.

http://www.underlandpress.com

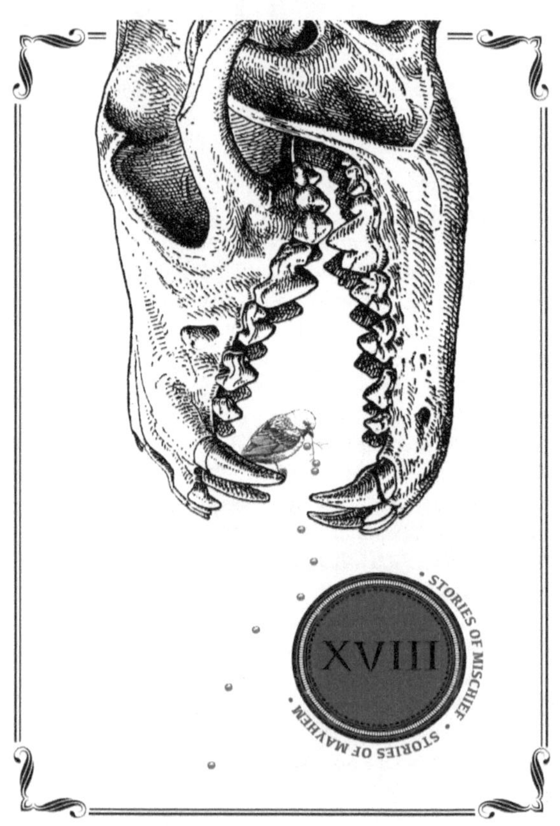

XVIII
STORIES OF MISCHIEF · STORIES OF MAYHEM

XVIII

The eighteenth Tarot card is the Moon, and those who raise their arms to her know she offers Mercy and Severity in equal measure. This is the great river at night, where wolves howl and all doors are open. All futures are possible, and every truth is elusive. This is the source and passion of *Eighteen: Stories of Mischief & Mayhem*. These twenty-four stories from voices—old and new—celebrate the inevitability of fate, the horror of prophecy, and the shivering delight of not knowing what comes next.

Cross over the threshold with us, and explore the strange, the weird, and the fantastic. Do not fear what lies ahead. It is the same as what came before. The only difference is you. This is *Eighteen*, and nothing will be the same.

With stories by Forrest Aguirre • Darin Bradley • Christopher East • Scott Edelman • Nicole Feldringer • Ben Gamblin • Ingrid Garcia • A. P. Howell • Emma Johnson-Rivard • E. E. King • Jessie Kwak • Shannon Lawrence • Gerri Leen • Mark Mills • Christi Nogle Tammie Painter • Josh Rountree • Erica Sage • Lorraine Schein • J. Dee Stanley • Richard Thomas • John Waterfall • Wendy N. Wagner • Todd Zack

Edited by Mark Teppo.

Available at independent bookstores everywhere.

http://www.underlandpress.com